# FLEETING

## THE NASH BROTHERS, BOOK ONE

## CARRIE AARONS

*To the woman who feels unanchored ... may you relish the freedom.*

Do you want your **FREE** Carrie Aarons eBook?

All you have to do is **<u>sign up for my newsletter</u>**, and you'll immediately receive your free book!

# 1

"This is probably the most embarrassing doctor's visit I've ever had. And it's not even for me."

Looking down at my grandmother's four-year-old dog, Chance, I try to give him my best stink-eye. It's a well-trained expression of mine, and it must work, because his big brown eyes, at least, hold some guilt as he drags his butt on the ground.

I have to physically pull him up the brick steps by his leash and onto the porch of the veterinarian's office, which doesn't look like an office at all. The building that houses the pet doctor is a Victorian home, with maroon shutters and dark blue whimsical trim that makes it look more like an old-school carousel than a place to treat sick animals.

The bell over the door jingles as I turn the antique brass knob to the front door, and I'm greeted by the smell of fresh cotton and lingering dog hair.

A pretty, older woman with gray hair in floral scrubs sits behind a white-washed desk, her hands flying over a keyboard as she talks to someone on the other end of the phone.

"Dr. Nash has a surgery tomorrow, but he can come up and

see the horse on Thursday. Just keep at it with a lot of water, and if you don't see improvement, you know the after-hours number. All right, you too, Martha. Okay, thanks, see you then."

She looks up at me after finishing the note on her screen and smiles. A genuine, pearly-white grin ... to me, a complete stranger. It's something I haven't gotten used to in the three weeks I've been living in Fawn Hill, Pennsylvania. The rural *niceness* of this community is so foreign to my New York City mindset. You can't pull a girl out of six years of living among urbanites who are rude on arrival and expect her to take genuine caring at face value.

"Hi, there, how can I help you?" She looks down at Chance, the boxer practically frowning at her. "Oh, Chance, dear, we meet again. You must be Presley, Hattie McDaniel's granddaughter. It's nice to meet you."

Her steamrolling of the conversation catches me off guard. That's the other thing about living in a small town, everyone knows who you are and who you're related to, even if they've never seen your face.

"Uh, hi. Yes, Chance here ... he ate something he shouldn't have, and I think it's ... stuck. I called about twenty minutes ago." My face heats even though I don't mention exactly *what* he swallowed.

"Oh, yes, dear, I forgot! We've had such a busy morning. A horse is sick up at the Dennis' barn, and just this morning Dr. Nash has seen two cats with incontinence issues, and a rabbit with a broken tooth. It sure is a funny farm around here!"

I'm not sure what to say to this, and Chance whimpers where he sits next to me. "So, can the doctor see him?"

The receptionist stands from her desk, still smiling. "Of course, Chance is a frequent flyer. It'll be another minute or two. I'm Dierdra, by the way. Gosh, I'm sure glad you came to town to help your grandmother. With her sight, it's a wonder she's been able to keep the shop going."

I get the feeling that Dierdra is a bit of a gossip, but a well-meaning one. "Thank you, yes, I'm glad I could move here to help her."

"Have you eaten at Kip's Diner, yet? Best pie in this part of the state although it's a bit of a hidden gem. The whole of Fawn Hill is, really."

She laughs jovially, and I feel myself warming to her. She might be a bit chatty, but her kindness puts me at ease. And she's right, because since I've been here, I realized I needed a bit of Fawn Hill medicine.

Not that we'd visited a lot growing up, because Dad moved away from his hometown right after high school and didn't look back. But the two times we'd made the trip from Albany to Grandma's house for Christmas, I'd marveled at the storybook community she lived in. Fawn Hill was the quintessential small town, a gem of farmhouses and Victorian homes situated on either side of Main Street. The backdrop of the Welsh Mountains dotted the skyline, and the children here still walked to the singular elementary, middle, and high schools the town boasted.

It was picturesque, quiet living, and it wasn't a mystery what my grandmother loved so much about it. Even if I missed the bustle of the city, I could appreciate Fawn Hill for its charm.

"I haven't yet, but now I'm going to wrangle my grandma into buying me a slice of apple." I nod at her.

Chance excites when another owner walks through the door with a small, tan dog. I have to brace myself as he almost pulls my arm out of its socket and barking ensues.

Behind me, a door clicks shut, and Dierdra is talking to someone as I try to rein in Chance.

"Presley, Dr. Nash will see Chance now."

A lock of my hair is caught in my mouth as I finally turn,

breathing hard with the leash looped seven times around my wrist so I can keep my grandmother's mongrel from friendly attacking the other patients.

"Come on in."

*Holy crap.* Why didn't anyone warn me that Fawn Hill also had the hottest veterinarian I've ever seen? Talk about a hidden gem.

A tall drink of water with dirty blond hair, eyes the color of my favorite dark chocolate swirled with caramel, muscled thighs that couldn't possibly belong to a doctor and a smile that could charm the pants off of Simon Cowell.

Okay, I'd been watching too much *America's Got Talent*.

"You're Dr. Nash?" My voice held a tone of skeptical rudeness, and I cringed at myself. "You just ... look so ... young."

What I'd meant to say was hot ... *you're way too hot to be a vet.* This guy had sex hair, the kind you grabbed onto while he slowly stoked your fire. He looked straitlaced, a little too good-boy for my taste, but with those chiseled cheekbones and cleft chin, a girl would be blind not to feel that familiar tingle south of the border when he turned those mocha eyes on her.

But instead of the word sexy, I'd said the word young instead, and now he was giving me an amused raised eyebrow.

And then I remembered why I was here.

*Oh my God.* This gorgeous specimen is going to be responsible for pulling my hot pink lace underwear out of this damn dog's butt.

# 2

---

KEATON

She was clearly uncomfortable.

"Chance, my man, we have to stop meeting like this."

I pat the dog's head as he sits on my exam room floor, his tongue lolling as I scratch behind his ear.

"This dog is a menace." The woman sneers.

I look up at her and can't stop myself from staring for the hundredth time since we came into this room. It's just ... she's stunning.

Red hair the color of crushed cherries, a lithe frame with long, toned legs encased in black yoga pants, and cleavage that keeps peeking out from her white tank top. With hair like that, you'd expect freckles, but I have a feeling nothing about this woman is *usual*. No, her skin is a rose-petal blush melted with vanilla ice cream, smooth and completely blemish free.

And those eyes. Emerald green and hypnotic, even when they're rolling at the menace panting in my face.

"He's just a little overexcited. Nothing a little training wouldn't fix up, or so I keep telling Hattie. I'm Keaton, by the way." I extend my hand, hoping she'll give me her name.

"I thought it was Dr. Nash." She gives me an unreadable

expression, cautiously extending her hand but not giving me her name.

I chuckle. "I'm a vet in small-town Pennsylvania. If I walked around here asking everyone to call me Dr. Nash, they'd think I was a stuck-up prick."

This wins me a laugh, and when she smiles, something inside of my chest pulls. Like a muscle that hasn't been used in a while, the soreness hurts but is also satisfying.

"Down-to-earth doctor ... I don't hate it. I've met many who wouldn't allow anyone in a town like this to even shine their shoes." Nameless minx smiles.

"Fawn Hill may be small, but its people have heart. It's a loyal, wonderful town." I defend the place I've lived my entire life.

She holds up her hands. "Oh no, please don't mistake that for criticism on your town. On the contrary, it's a slight at doctors. I used to work in a restaurant close to a hospital. Those assholes don't tip nearly as well as they're getting paid to cut into people."

I tilt my head, wondering where this restaurant was. But I settle with my earlier question. "Well, I know you're Hattie's granddaughter. But I still don't know your name."

She finally relents, sighing as if she's lost a battle. "I'm Presley, thanks for fitting us in on such short notice."

My attention focuses back on Chance, who is whining and dragging his butt on the ground. "No problem, as I said, I'm familiar with his case. Now, let's see if you can't hold him still in a hug while I see what he's eaten this time."

Presley's sharp cheekbones pink, and I notice the flush move down her neck. My eyes stray, and I wonder idly if her skin is this creamy everywhere.

*Get it together, doc.*

I shake my head, instructing her how to hold Chance so he

doesn't wiggle. All the while, she clamps her lips shut, and I'm confused. With gloves secured, I move to the dog's back end, lifting his tail to inspect the damage he's done.

The evidence of a bowel movement is there, but by the way he's whimpering and moving, I can tell that whatever he ate is wrapped in there good.

"Do you have any idea what it might be? Just don't want to reach in there if it may be sharp. I could hurt him, and myself." I look at Presley across Chance's back.

She's kneeling on the floor holding him, and how she makes it look so elegant, I have no idea. "Um, well, it must have been a few days ago, because he's been having a hard time this morning ..."

It probably wasn't anything dangerous to the dog if he'd gone a few days with it in his system. This was part of my job I, obviously, did not enjoy, but somebody had to stick their hand up an animal's butt to help the poor guys out.

I try to make light of it as my hand moves. "Didn't think you'd be in for such excitement when you moved to Fawn Hill, huh?"

Presley's full peach lips tug up in a small smile, but she's still wearing that look of worry. Maybe she's concerned about Chance?

It takes a few minutes of gentle tugging, but I finally help the dog out, and go to the garbage and sink to clean off.

"What is ... this?" I ask as the water runs over the material in my hands.

"Oh God ..." Presley's plea is a whisper, and when I turn, I see one hand over her eyes.

And if I'm not mistaken, that raspy voice is full of embarrassment.

Turning back to my hand in the sink, the object becomes clear.

It's a pair of hot pink lace underwear, cut thong style.

"Oh ... I ... well ..." I stutter, completely unprofessionally.

I just had my hand up her dog's butt, and I'm blushing over a pair of sexy underwear. *Real great bedside manner, Keaton.*

"Who knew that Chance and I had the same taste in thongs?" Presley laughs sheepishly.

I swear, my balls tingle when she says the word thong. What the hell is wrong with me?

"One time, I had a goat that ate its owner's vibrator."

The minute I say it, I know I'm in deep shit, literally, when it comes to this woman. I never lose control or get struck by word vomit. I'm Mr. Dependable, the amiable, boring one ... according to my brothers.

Presley's eyes go wide, and then she keels over, laughing hysterically until her breath comes out in gasps. She laughs as if the very act is going out of style, and I can't help the smile that splits my face watching her.

"How did the goat even get a vibrator? I can't even imagine, and I think I'm embarrassed!"

I grin. "They keep it in the house as a pet. Don't go spreading that around, I'm supposed to keep that whole doctor-patient confidentiality thing."

"Oh, I doubt the goat will find out." She winks.

And my heart beats twice, rapidly enough that I have to clutch a hand onto the collared polo at my neck. I haven't felt it do this in ... two whole years. An instant flash of pain follows the beats because that's what the organ is trained to do.

My smile fades and I snap off my gloves, bending down to pat Chance on the head again.

"He's all set. Welcome to town, Presley. I hope you can learn to see the beauty in Fawn Hill." I keep it professional.

Flirting with a woman who loosens all of my control so quickly, without much more than her name and her preference of pink thongs to go on, is dangerous. I don't need that kind of complication in my life, especially with everything that is already on my plate.

She frowns, I'm sure at my split-second change in mood. "Thanks. How much do I owe you?"

I turn to scribble in Chance's chart, avoiding eye contact. "It's on the house. Just tell Hattie to get him into training."

# 3

Pull out of my office driveway onto Main Street, take a right on Horsham Road, a left on Woodfield Avenue and continue driving until the pavement becomes gravel.

About half a mile after that, you'll reach Nash Trail, aptly named by my father when he built the house he would later raise a family in.

The big yellow farmhouse wasn't actually on a farm although my parents' acreage was nothing to laugh at. They'd settled in Fawn Hill over thirty years ago, before my brothers and I were even born, and Mom had loved this style of home so much that my dad built her dream for her. Two floors, brick and shiplap exterior, with white columns studding the wraparound porch.

With four boys, they needed the six acres their property sat on. My brothers and I almost burned the house down three times, crashed six cars between us, broke bones left and right, and were regularly menaces.

The word reminds me of Presley McDaniel, and I have to pause as I turn the engine off. Her face, all of that thick, red hair

... it had plagued my mind for the rest of the week. On my daily outings for lunch, I'd purposely avoided anything left of my office, knowing I could probably see her through the window of her grandmother's bookstore that doubled as the town post office.

I shake my head, focusing on walking into my parents' house, the American flag my father hung years ago waving over the detached garage.

The house I grew up in was picturesque, as was my childhood. And when I was old enough, I took over my father's veterinary practice. My grandparent's only had enough money to send Dad for his vet tech certification as a teenager ... college just wasn't a thing they could afford. He helped out in Fawn Hill's existing practice and put himself through night and weekend veterinary school until I was about eight years old, when he became a full-fledged doctor. I remember his graduation; how proud he looked, how Mom cried, and how cool it was to see my last name plastered on the sign outside the vet's office.

I inherited his love for animals, and when the time came, my parents helped put me through college. The unspoken agreement, as his oldest son, was that I would follow in his footsteps and take over his practice. Good thing I never wanted to do anything else, although from time to time, I wondered if my life would be completely different if I hadn't toed the line.

Sighing, I get out of the car, knowing that instead of the quiet beer on my couch I crave, I'll be walking into noise and nagging.

As soon as I push through the red front door, which only reminds me of a certain stranger's hair, I'm bombarded.

"Woah, dude, way to be late. At least it's not me. Hey, Ma, I'm not the last one here!" Fletcher, my youngest brother, calls out as he pops a piece of cheese in his mouth.

He walks away, not even bothering to say hi or ask how my day was. *Here we go.*

I didn't mean to be cranky; I loved my brothers, but since my father's sudden passing two years ago, I felt more like a parent than a peer a lot of the time.

And there it was. The reason why I felt so ... *off* every time I arrived for Friday night dinner. My mother still insisted on the tradition, but I always expected to walk in and hear his booming laugh. Who knew that a healthy, recently retired man could die of a heart attack on a Sunday in July?

Certainly none of us. My family hadn't been the same since, though we all put on the front that things were all hunky-dory.

The pain, that sharp, poisonous stab of agony, is still fresh in all of my internal organs as I walk through the house. My heart, my gut, my mind and everything in between sours as my shoes tread the same carpet that my father did. He was my hero, my role model, and I don't say those things lightly. The man had integrity and knowledge; he gave love and affection freely to his boys even if it wasn't the most manly of things.

Perhaps his passing spurred this need to be alone in me. He'd done everything right, had been the picture of a family man. And the world took that away from him, way too early. What would it do to me?

"Oh, Keaton, sweetheart, you're here!" My mom was stirring a pot on the stove, and I went over to kiss her cheek as she stuck it out for me to greet her.

"The golden child graces us with his presence." Forrest rolls his eyes as he sets plates out on the table we've been eating at since I was five.

Forrest and Fletcher are twins, and six years younger than I am. Forrest is older by a minute, something he never lets our brother forget, and they both still make just as much trouble as they did when they were ten.

Although, they do it in different ways. Forrest just received his fourth warning from the state police department to stop hacking into things he shouldn't, except they've also extended two job positions so he doesn't take the warnings seriously. He's the county's only forensic detective, and the kid is a goddamn genius, not that I'd tell him that. It would only go further to his head.

Fletcher walks in, cradling a beer, and by the gait in his step, I know it's not his first. My baby brother could be just as successful as his twin, but of all of us, he has the biggest weakness. Alcohol is his crutch, his weapon, his medicine, and his addiction. I've tried twice to get him sober, and they've both ended in him not speaking to me for months. I'm afraid of what is going to happen if we don't all intervene soon.

"Sorry, I run my own office." Opening the fridge, I grab a beer and use an opener to flip the top off, taking a long pull.

"Always rubbing the business owner card in our face. Ever think that some of us are happier as worker bees?" Fletcher laughs.

He's currently on his fifth job, and second auto body shop, since graduating high school six years ago.

"Boys, stop it. Can we just have one nice Friday night dinner with no teasing?" Mom scolds us, and we all shut up.

My mother is petite, more than a foot shorter than all of her boys, with dark hair and darker eyes. She's a third Native American and her looks prove it. We're all a mix of our parents, except for me, the only one with Mom's eyes. Their dark brown hair mixed with translucent blue eyes, courtesy of our father, don't quite match my dark eyes and dirty blond hair.

"Listen to your mother."

A deep, annoyed voice sharply snaps from the doorway.

Bowen, the middle child, walks in, still in his boots and apron.

"Hybrid, much, Bowie?" Forrest chuckles.

"Shut up, Jungle." Bowen flips him the bird and sits down next to me.

The nicknames never stop when you grow up among four immature boys.

"Did you have a call today?" I take in the boots dirtying Mom's floor under the table.

He nods, stealing my beer. "A small electrical fire a couple miles from town, before you reach the highway. Had to close up shop to respond."

By day, Bowen owned the barber shop in Fawn Hill. And by other day, and some nights, he was one of the only four volunteer firefighters we had.

"Everything go okay?" I scowl at my pilfered drink.

He nods. "Yep."

Bowen is a man of few words, but we were closer with each other than we were with the twins. We were only two years apart, we'd grown up in tandem, and no one would ever have the bond Forrest and Fletcher did.

"All right, come help bring the food to the table," Mom hollers and we all jump up.

"Thanks for cooking, Mom." Bowen kisses our mother as he picks up a bowl of mashed potatoes, and she pats his arm.

"You know, there is nothing I like better than sitting down to a meal with my boys." The sadness in her eyes for the person missing from this dinner table is unmistakable.

"Mom, did you get to the library this week?" I try to distract her.

She nods, as the serving dishes are set on the table, and we begin to dig in. "I did, helped Lily put away the new shipment of children's books. They are just so darling, all of those little card-board-bound stories. If only I had a grandchild to read them to."

Her sigh echoes around the table, and none of us are

touching *that* with a six-foot pole. She's been dropping the line for a year now, telling us that the family is lonely and needs some happiness and why doesn't just one of us settle down already.

Fletch is shoveling meatloaf into his mouth while Forrest sneaks looks at his cell phone in his lap. Bowen is being typical Bowen, looking angrily off into space as if the whole world has offended him.

"I had to retrieve a pair of pink underwear from a dog's butt today," I say, hoping to break the tension.

Almost everyone at the table lets out a laugh, and I launch into the story, welcoming the hilarious distraction.

The only thing I leave out is the saucy redhead who won't seem to leave my thoughts.

"Girl, how do you even have a high school diploma?"

Grandma chides me as she rips the packaging envelope from my hands, shaking her head so that the white-gray curls cut close to her scalp bounce.

"I'm just getting used to the machine, that's all," I grumble, chastising myself on top of her insult.

Working a postage machine shouldn't be this hard, but I've never used one and Grandma's teaching about any process is usually one clipped sentence that makes no sense. Thus, I'm left to figure almost everything out on my own, which ends in mistakes and her criticism.

This won't work for long since the whole reason I moved to Fawn Hill was to take a majority of the responsibility at McDaniel's Books & Post. Grandma had started the shop with my grandfather when they were newly married at the age of eighteen, back when you couldn't buy books on the Internet or print out your own packing slips. The store doubled as both a place to buy novels and a center for all shipping, mailing, copying and any other business needs. Honestly, the concept was kind of genius, and McDaniel's was the only post office in a twenty-five-mile radius, so Grandma did well for herself.

Until this fall when the doctor diagnosed her with debilitating glaucoma. She'd had an operation, after which my dad, her son, had come to town to care for her. But the surgery hadn't worked like they'd hoped it would, and she was essentially losing more of her vision daily. She needed someone to help her out at home and in the shop. I don't know what made me volunteer one random afternoon when Dad had called to ask how my, multiple, jobs were going, but I had.

Maybe I'd needed an out from my crappy life in New York. Maybe I needed to prove something to my family ... that they could count on me. Maybe I wanted to spend more time with the grandmother who'd been so much of a mystery to me growing up.

Either way, here I was. With said grandmother bossing me around as I messed up time after time in her store.

The bell over the door jingled, and a petite woman with dark hair, almond-shaped eyes, and a kind smile walked to the counter holding a small package.

"Hello, how can I help you?" I asked her.

Grandma came bustling out of the back supply room, her sturdy, thin body hustling around. "Oh, Eliza, hello!"

The woman who had just walked in, Eliza I guess, smiled wider. "Hattie! Good to see you, how are you feeling?"

"Well, those damn doctors keep trying to off me, but here I am. And if this one would learn quicker, I'd be able to retire." Grandma rolled her eyes at me.

My blood pressure shot up. No one said anything about her retiring since my stay here wasn't permanent. But hell ... what did I think? I couldn't just help for a while and think her blindness was going to reverse itself. Yet, I hadn't thought about it until this very moment.

Was I really going to stay and live my life in Fawn Hill?

"This must be your granddaughter. I'd heard she was in town but haven't had the pleasure yet. Hi, I'm Eliza Nash, it's so nice to meet you."

Nash, huh? I studied her as she set her package down on the counter between us. Yes, she did look like him. The eyes mostly, but the man I'd met almost a week ago must be her son.

"Presley McDaniel, it's nice to meet you." I smiled back.

Small-town niceness was slowly working its way into my blood.

"Eliza here has four boys; all live in town. You met her oldest, the vet, Dr. Nash, when Chance ate your underwear the other day." Grandma pats me on the back.

Eliza lets out a laugh. "That was Chance? I should have suspected, the troublemaker. Keaton told us about that over Friday night dinner."

A vision of what her family table must look like on a Friday night popped into my head, and before I could stop the thought, I wondered if the handsome doctor had a wife. Did they hold hands as he told his mother the unfortunate poop problems of my grandmother's dog?

"Keaton is a good egg, that one. Shame he hasn't been snatched up, yet." Grandma eyes me, a devilish twinkle in our matching green pools.

The woman has a sixth freaking sense; I swear.

His mother sighs. "You have no idea how much I long for a daughter-in-law. If just one of them would settle down and give me a handful of grandbabies, I'd be complete. The house has just been so lonely since Jack passed."

Her sadness is palpable, and my heart hurts for her. I don't even know her, but I can tell from the droop of her eyes that she lost someone very close to her.

Grandma walks around the counter and squeezes a

supportive arm around her shoulders. "I know how you feel. Since Lester went to heaven, it hasn't been the same. But we're still here, and we have to try to carry on."

This woman must have lost her husband, I realize, because she wears the same look of grief as my grandmother, who lost her husband five years ago.

Eliza sniffles and nods then perks up. "Gosh, excuse me. I didn't come in here to break down. I came to mail this package to my sister in Connecticut."

"Well, good thing you did, because Presley here just started to fly solo and she can help you with whatever you need." Grandma gives me an encouraging look, which fills me with confidence.

Even though she teases me, and can be rough around the edges, my grandmother has shown more pride in me than my parents have in my entire life. Not that I had anything resembling a tough childhood, and I love my parents, but as the middle child, I've never been doted on per se. I've never had the drive or talent like my older sister or younger brother, and the members of my family usually count on me to screw up.

Grandma is giving me a chance, and my chest fills with determination to prove her right.

"I certainly can. Would you like to send this via USPS, Fed Ex or UPS?" I start with my questions, trying to follow the steps my grandmother walked me through.

Eliza asks me how much it will be for each, so she can weigh her options. Using the computer behind the counter, I let her know, and once she picks the postal service, I put in her details and print the label, sticking it on her package. Then I ring her up, make the sale, and smile once she's told me she doesn't require anything further.

"I think you have the perfect new owner, Hattie." Eliza grins at me.

Is it strange that I'm so proud of myself for correctly preparing a package for shipping? Who am I?

"We'll see." Grandma's brows draw together, but I see the smirk she's trying to conceal.

"Presley, it was very nice to meet you. I hope we see you soon, maybe at the Summer Kickoff Carnival next weekend? My boys and I always run the caramel corn booth."

How very quaint and adorable that sounded. And I had to bite my own tongue to keep from drooling when I thought about hot Dr. Nash and caramel in the same sentence.

"Sure, it's not like I've got other plans in Fawn Hill." I shrug.

She leaves after a brief conversation with Grandma, which I can't hear since they're by the door.

"Come on, chicken legs, let's go get some dinner," Grandma says, walking behind the counter to close the till and shut down the computers.

"Where do you want to go?" Picking up some scattered boxes and packaging materials, I help her clean and straighten so that we leave the shop pristine.

"Not even a question, we're going to Kip's. Can't get a better slice of pie anywhere within a hundred miles. Plus, if you know who to ask, they have fresh-baked Amish bread behind the counter. Get ready for some carbs, my dear."

Sounded like a great night to me.

After closing up shop, we walk the two blocks to Kip's Diner, which is bustling even on a Tuesday night. When I walk in behind Grandma, almost every table turns to say hello, and there are a number of people who shout "Hattie!" across the restaurant. Families with little children, older couples, and throngs of teenagers fill the booths. Motown music puts a jovial tune in the atmosphere, and I'm instantly charmed. Plus, whatever that smell is coming from the kitchen, it's making my mouth water.

We sit in a corner booth in the back, and I get the feeling that they keep this open just for my grandmother. Our waitress, a bright-eyed brunette teenager, greets her and asks if she wants the regular.

"Yes, dear. My regular cheeseburger with Colby-jack, extra pickles, onion rings on the side and a nice, cold glass of iced tea. And bring some of that Amish bread out before our meal, I want my granddaughter to try it."

The girl nods and looks to me. "I'll have the same."

Whatever Grandma orders must be good, so I just go with it.

I look out the window as she collects the menus and walks away, watching the late May sun descend over the buildings on Main Street. It really is a cute little town, with its pretty store-fronts and brick buildings positioned between rolling green hills and mountains.

"See something you like?" Grandma interrupts my thoughts.

I smile, shaking my head. "Just looking."

"See *anyone* you like?" She winks, waving a hand over the diner.

I can't help turning my head, looking around the diner to see if a certain pet doctor was there. "Subtle, Grandma. But no, I don't have time for that."

"A young, beautiful fox like you doesn't have time for passion or love? Then I must have one foot in the grave if I see some faces I'd like to get to know."

Rolling my eyes, I can't help the laugh that bursts forth. "You're shameless. But my life is all over the place, it would be unfair to invite someone into this chaos."

Our waitress sets delicious-smelling bread down in front of us, and I drool at the steam coming off of it.

"Hmm, seems to me you might be able to find some roots here," Grandma says this quietly, almost willing my thoughts to consider making this move permanent.

"Stop messing with me, you old coot." I shoot her a perfectly practiced stink eye.

She chuckles and breaks off a piece of bread. "It's fun having you around, kid. Makes me feel young again. Makes me feel like I might get you into some trouble."

I had a feeling she might be right about that second part, and I was a little scared and a little excited to find out what said trouble was.

L iving in a small town has its advantages.

Everyone knows your name. People are friendly. It's not hard to find anything. The taxes are cheaper. There is a sense of inclusiveness.

But with everything, there are disadvantages.

Everyone knows your name and your occupation. Which leads to many people thinking you'll give them a discount because you went to high school together, or because their mother donated to your brother's marathon fundraiser, or some other thing.

People are friendly, which leads to nosiness, which often means every single person in town will ask why you aren't married yet. I won't even tell you how many times I've been asked why I don't just find a nice girl.

And that sense of inclusiveness? Sometimes, you just want to be alone. A nameless face in a sea of thousands.

I don't mean to be a downer, because I truly love Fawn Hill and my friends and family, but it's just been one of those days. I had a dog die on my table this morning and then got a call from a local farmer that his horse lost the foal she was carrying. To top it off, Dierdra forgot to make confirmation calls to today's patients, so three out of my four wellness visits didn't show up, and I spilled coffee in my car.

Which is why I did a stupid thing.

Generally, I am as in-the-lines as they come. I go to work; I pay my taxes early; I call my grandparents weekly and always use the crosswalk. I don't color outsides the lines; I don't break rules or promises, to myself or others. I'm predictable and boring, as I've been told a thousand times by Fletcher, and I like it that way.

I'd been good for two weeks about not allowing myself to go into McDaniel's Books & Post. I already had a crush on Presley McDaniel, one that I'd been denying since she came into my practice. There was no good that could come from crushing harder on her. She was a nomad, and there was no way a woman like that was settling in Fawn Hill.

Except, as I was walking back from getting a mid-afternoon coffee at Fawn Hill Java, my mind went haywire and threw my carefully constructed rule book out the window. Before I knew what was happening, the bell over the door was tinkling as I crossed the threshold, and then there she was.

Presley straightened up from where she'd been slouching over a book on the counter. Her sunset-colored hair was piled high on top of her head today, leaving her face unframed. I could see the high slant of her cheekbones and the way that all of those long lashes kissed her cheeks when they hooded over those green eyes. She looks comfortable yet put-together in her short-sleeved sundress, and I'm rewarded with a brief smile as I walk through the door.

"Reading on the job?" I hope that opening line is okay.

It's been so long since I've felt the urge to flirt that I'm probably completely rusty.

Presley looks down at the book and flaps the front cover over to mark her spot, then closes it.

"It's slow this time of day. The morning rush of postal carriers and UPS drivers is done, and the lunch chaos of workers trying to mail letters is over. Now I just have to wait for the onslaught of after-school mom's trying to mail same-day packages, and it'll be time to close up shop."

I laugh at her accurate timetable of a normal day in Fawn Hill. "Sounds about right. Although dealing with animals is much less predictable than the Fawn Hill PTA. What are you reading?"

She holds it up so I can see the front cover, whose title is *The Perfect Couple*, written by Elin Hilderbrand. "It's fantastic, a little mystery, a mega beach read. I forgot how much I like reading, how a story can transport you to a different place entirely. I lost my love for books when I moved to New York City."

I walk farther into the shop and over to the counter to stand directly across from Presley. "I know what you mean. I'll read two or three great books and then get so busy that new ones start collecting dust on my nightstand. But when I come back to reading, I always remember how much I like it."

Presley nods like I'm speaking the exact thoughts she's thinking. "Yes! You're so right."

My fingers drum on the counter as I search for something to keep the conversation going. "Do you miss living in New York City?"

A thoughtful look passes over her face. "Hmm, well, I guess I miss the Chinese food you can order 'round the clock. And my yoga studio, gosh do I miss teaching classes. There isn't even a gym in Fawn Hill."

I don't miss the way her eyes light up when she mentions yoga. "You should talk to Lily at the library. They host cooking classes and other courses during the week, I'm sure they'd love if you mentioned teaching a yoga class."

Presley looks taken aback for a moment. "I ... I could do that, yeah."

Our conversation lapses for a moment, and I want to ask the obvious question burning in my throat.

"So is there anything else you miss?" There is no subtlety left in my voice. I am asking if she has someone she left back in New York.

She smiles like she knows what I'm trying to get at. "No, nothing else. I actually kind of like it here, which keeps surprising me. Oh, and I finally got a slice of pie at Kip's. They're either going to make me fat or take all my money. I'm not sure which will happen first."

"I won't tell you how many times I've had to loosen my belt on the afternoons I eat there."

And now I'm telling her about unbuckling my pants. Great. I have absolutely zero game.

But, Presley laughs, a tiny hint of pink stealing over her cheeks. "I don't doubt it."

And here it goes. I take a breath, my brain shouting at me to definitely not pass go and collect two hundred dollars. But my heart and my mouth tell that useless thought center they're doing it anyway.

"Maybe one afternoon I could take you out for a slice of pie? Or three?"

My heart is hammering in my chest, and I suddenly feel the need to drink a gallon of water. How stupid am I? I said I wasn't going to let my crush on this woman tempt me, and not twenty minutes into my second conversation with her, I'm asking her out. In a totally cheesy way, let's not forget. A slice of pie? I'm basically insinuating that I want to have sex with her. Which I do, but ...

*Shut up, doc.*

"Um ... yeah, sure. I'm kind of busy learning the ropes here, but maybe we could meet up in a couple of weeks."

And the slap of rejection burns across my cheeks. Ever wonder what it sounds like when a woman politely turns you down? Presley just gave the prime example.

"Great." I plaster a fake smile on my face. "That sounds great. Well, I've got to get back, have a guinea pig with a hiccup problem."

I start to walk out the door, but her voice stops me. "Oh, was there anything you needed help with in the shop?"

Fuck me. I walked in here and didn't even provide a cover for why I stopped in. I scramble, looking around, and pick up a random book off the shelf closest to me.

"I was going to buy this new book, but it will probably just collect dust on my nightstand. Thanks anyway!"

It's not until I'm almost out the door and can feel her hiding a smile behind my back, that I realize I just put back a children's sudoku puzzle book on the shelf.

# 6

*Oh my, the vet is adorable.*

I can't help the giggle that escapes my lips as I watch him speed walk back to his office, which is across the street and down three storefronts to the corner where the converted Victorian home sits. His deep breath before he asked me out. The fumbling, cheesy line about pie. The way his hands kept drumming on the counter. Keaton had been so nervous that I thought he might pass out before I could answer.

The sweet, *vanilla* Dr. Nash seemed like he'd make any number of these small-town girls the happiest person on the planet, but for me? We just weren't right. I felt like a bitch turning him down, especially with the roundabout no I gave as an answer, but he deserves someone much more together than me. He's a calm, blue-skied spring afternoon and I'm a tornado in the middle of a blizzard.

In the seconds after he asked, I almost said yes. Going out with the sexy vet in my new town would be fun. Hell, even if he couldn't hold a conversation, he was nice to look at. But he could hold a conversation, and a witty one at that. I think that's what ultimately made me say no. I was going to convince myself that we wouldn't fit because ... what if I ended up really liking him? I had no clue if I was staying here, or where I ultimately wanted my life to go. Getting involved with someone, especially someone as steady as Keaton Nash, was just asking for trouble.

My phone buzzes on the counter, and I lift it to see two messages waiting for me. I open the first.

Gwen: *How is Grandma? Tell her I send my love, but I'm working this weekend so I won't be able to call.*

I roll my eyes. So typical of my older sister to "send her love" in a text message that isn't even to our grandmother, and then casually drop in that she'll be doing important lawyer things this weekend so don't disrupt her. That's basically what the message was saying, and it infuriated me that even after twenty-seven years of knowing her narcissistic ways, she could still get to me.

Presley: *Grandma is good, I'll tell her.*

I left it short because I wasn't going to open the door for her to brag about work more than she already did. After a minute of waiting to see if she'll respond, and maybe ask about me, she doesn't, and I open the second message.

Ryan: *Hey, boo. How's it going in bumblefuck? Miss you, just had an iced macchiato and it made me think of you. Come home and I'll buy you one. I'll even spring for a seventeen-dollar martini at Al Pucco's.*

The smile that stretches my face is real, and a homesickness for my best friend and the city hits like a tidal wave. Although, I'd forgotten how expensive it all was. Seventeen bucks for a martini? I'd seen a sign outside the only bar on Main Street advertising three-dollar beers every weekday.

Presley: *Miss you more, lady. Surprisingly, bumblefuck ain't so bad. Very quiet, but they have three-dollar beer and the best pie I've ever eaten. How's the apartment? Your job? How's Daniel?*

Ryan and I lived together when I first moved to the Big Apple after college. We met at a spin class and fell in friendship love over organic avocado burgers. And now that I think about it, I kind of want to slap myself in the face for ever being that uppity. We shared an apartment for three years, until she moved in with her boyfriend, Daniel. He worked at a big Wall Street financial firm, and while I liked him okay, I couldn't really understand what Ryan saw in him. She was a smart-as-hell coder at one of the biggest social media companies in the world, ran triathlons, and had lived in London for half of her childhood. Compared to her, Daniel was drier than gluten-free bread.

Ryan: *Apartment is no more. Same with Daniel. He wanted to go to Florida for our summer vacation. I wanted to go to Madrid. It took me this long to see that the guy was dull as drywall. Who the hell wastes a year of their life for that?*

Presley: *Thank God, I don't know how many more times I could point out to you that the man ironed his socks. Good riddance. So, Madrid it is, then?*

Ryan: *I leave in two weeks, can't wait. My boss is going to let me work remotely for two months, so I'll be there for a while. A tryst with a Latin lover sounds like exactly the right dose of medicine to heal my stupid heart. Care to join me?*

Her life was so cool, and it made me jealous more than I wished to admit.

Presley: *Gotta pass this time, love. Have to stay here to help Grandma out. You should come visit, though. You might get a hoot out of this place. Plus, I'm thinking about hosting a yoga class. They don't have a studio here.*

Ryan: *Wait, you're going to start your own class? That's fucking awesome, Pres. Proud of you. Maybe I'll journey to bumblefuck after my European tour. Gotta get back to work, can't keep the masses from posting their most ridiculous inner thoughts. Love you.*

Presley: *Love you, more.*

Sighing, I set my phone down on the counter and start the procedure for locking up. I don't know why I'd randomly told her that I might start a yoga class. Keaton Nash had only told me about the library offerings less than half an hour ago. But the idea was flicking me in the forehead now, and wouldn't go away, like an annoying little brother.

I'd obviously noticed in the month I'd lived here that Fawn Hill didn't have a yoga studio, much less a gym. I'd been doing my practice on a yoga mat in Grandma's basement, and that was getting pretty old. It wasn't relaxing or soothing to move through sequences in a dank, moldy, unfinished room.

Maybe I'll check into the library classes like Keaton had mentioned. The worst the person running them could say was no. But, if they said yes, this might be something I could do for myself. It might be the start of something.

And wasn't it strange that the idea of building something here, of putting down roots in this small town, didn't have me sprinting in the other direction?

# 7

KEATON

Sun rays peak out from behind the clouds as my feet hit the pavement.

I rounded the bend on the far end of the lake at Bloomsbury Park, running steadily around the mile-long track paved into the shores of the town's only body of water. Sweat trickled from my brows ... for the first week of June, it was humid and hot even at eight in the morning. My calves ached and the knee I'd hyperextended playing baseball in high school screamed at me. But I kept going. The burn in my lungs felt cathartic, and running is one of the only activities that takes me out of my own head.

My life might not look stressful, living in a small town as a single guy, but the responsibility on my shoulders was, at times, crushing. I ran my own veterinary practice. Aside from Dierdra answering the phones and keeping the schedule, and my accountant looking at my books every quarter, I did most everything else. I saw patients, operated, birthed farm animals, ordered supplies, ran our small social media presence, participated in community events, and volunteered at the county shelter twice a month.

And that was just my job. I was also the oldest child, and with Dad gone, the man of the family. When Mom had trouble with her gutters, or car, or needed something out of the attic, or ... anything really, I was the one she called. Reliable, steady Keaton, that was me. When my brothers were in trouble, I was the one who fixed the problem. I wrangled them on the holidays, scolded them when they didn't do what they'd promised Mom, and was the moral compass of the Nash family.

It was exhausting. And October, the third anniversary of Dad's death, was only four months away. Which meant the stress was only going to intensify.

Mom was going to go into complete mourning, just like she had the year before. It had lasted until well after New Year's when I'd finally threatened her with therapy that she'd refused many times before.

But she was going to have a bigger problem this year. My brothers and I agreed that she couldn't stay in the six-bedroom house we'd grown up in. It was too big, too much maintenance, and every single corner and closet reminded her of our father. I loved the house almost as much as she did, but on the upcoming third year since his passing, it was time to let it go.

We all had to start living again.

I headed into mile four, my arms pumping to the music blasting through my headphones. Coming out here on a weekday morning was my favorite time, almost no other Fawn Hill resident took to running the lake path at this time.

My phone rings from the band wrapped around my arm, cutting The Who off. I slow down, taking it out of its sleeve. The number that flashes on the screen turns the blood in my veins to ice. Because there can only be one reason *he's* calling, and even if his reaching out does me a favor, he's still the last person on earth I want to talk to.

"Gerry, is he there?" I pick up, letting him know I know why he's calling.

A grunt and what sounds like glass crunching in the background. "Yeah, he's here. Better get down here quick, Keaton, or I'll be forced to call the cops if he tries to take his keys."

"Fucking, hell," I say more to myself than to Gerry Flint.

Gerry Flint is the owner of the Goat & Barrister, the one bar on Main Street. He's a decent man, but with the history between us, we're never going to be friends.

His daughter had bashed my heart in with a bat ... and even if we'd been chummy once, there was no coming back from that.

Sprinting to the parking lot, I'm peeling out and swerving through town in a frenzy. Two cars actually honk at me on my way to the bar, and road rage is unheard of in our town.

Within five minutes of the phone call, I'm walking into the Goat. It's a dark tavern, with wood paneling and old British-inspired decor. The person Gerry called about is slumped over the sticky, cherry-top bar, but I can tell he isn't sleeping.

"Fletcher." I sigh, not knowing if his name is a curse, a question or simply a resigned greeting.

My brother looks up, his eyes glassy, a cut above his lip bleeding, and then turns back to Gerry, who is polishing glasses behind the bar.

"You called him, you asshole? I don't need a daddy, or didn't you hear mine is dead?" Fletch practically spits at the owner, and I cringe.

"That's enough, Fletch. Let's go, I'll drive you home. Gerry, thank you for calling. Can I have his keys? We'll pick his car up later."

There was smashed glass under his chair, and I could see beer dripping from a poster over a table on the other wall. As I neared, I caught a whiff of Fletcher and had to hold my breath. He'd definitely pissed himself, and it was possible there was throw up on his T-shirt. Fuck, and I was going to let him in my car?

My youngest brother ... the family addict. I blew out a breath, trying to hold my temper at bay. Fletch had always been a party boy, he was the one you called for a good time. When Dad was alive, he kept it under wraps more ... although Bowen and I had been the ones to bail him out of jail twice; once when he was eighteen and once when he was twenty, both for being drunk and disorderly. It got worse after that, and when I still lived at home, I'd find liquor bottles hidden in all sorts of places. The year after Dad died, he got a DUI and had been forced into an out-patient rehab as part of his court sentence. That had lasted all of six months, and he'd been slowly drinking himself to death since.

"I can drive." He pushes my hand away when I try to help lift him off the stool. "Hey, get your hands off me, pussy!"

I don't consider myself to have a short fuse, on the contrary mine's probably pretty long, but I've had it with Fletcher. I know he's an addict, and I know it's a disease, but when you're in it, watching a family member ruin their life, it's hard not to get angry.

"I said, let's fucking go. Or would you rather I call the cops on you, brother?" I bite out.

Fletcher cracks up laughing, his body swaying as he stands. "Oh, man, I ruffled Keaton's feathers, I'm in *big* trouble!"

He cackles, poking my chest. "I'm not scared of you, big brother, and I'm definitely more fun than you. Not all of us want to live our lives celibate with our collar buttoned up to our eyeballs."

My blood was boiling, sending hurricane waves crashing in my ears, and I had to bite my fingernails into my palms to stop from snapping his head back with a good sucker punch.

Instead, I grabbed his elbow and pulled him across the bar,

past Gerry, who calls out as I'm about to push the door open into the sunny street outside.

"You need to do something about that, Keaton. Sooner or later, he's going to kill himself. Or someone else."

His tone hits a nerve in me, and I turn with my hand still wrapped around my brother's elbow so he can't bolt for the door. "You're the one who served him until the early hours of the morning!"

Gerry shrugs. "It's a business, Nash. I'm a bartender, not a nurse or his mama."

That snaps my patience. "Don't tell me how to take care of my family, Gerry. You raised a daughter who left behind a good life, both with me and with you. Don't act like you know how to influence or control someone any better than I can. As I recall, you asked her to reconsider her choice, and she still left. So don't tell me how to handle my business."

The man's face falls, but his upper-lip stiffens. "Boy, if you don't realize by now that she did you a favor, you're a moron. You weren't right for each other, we all saw it. Get your romantic head out of your ass and get over it. And get out of my bar. I don't want to see your brother in here again."

My gut burns as I push out of the bar, the sun forcing me to squint. Just an hour ago, I'd relished taking in the early morning rays, and the fresh smell of the day.

"Don't bring me home. Mom can't know. Please, Keat," Fletcher begs me, and a part of me sympathizes with him.

Somewhere in my brain, I know he can't help the way he is. And I also don't want to subject our poor mother to this.

"I'll bring you to Bowen's, but just know he's going to kick your ass when he gets home."

Now, with my sick, broken brother leaning on my shoulder at eight a.m., I can't wait for this shit day to be over already.

"Stir that caramel. And don't give me that look, asshole. You're silent today, remember?"

Bowen's voice is clipped as he orders Fletcher around, but I'm too damn hot to notice. It has to be about a thousand degrees in this tent, and I wonder for the tenth year in a row, why we allow Mom to force us into manning the caramel corn booth at the Summer Kickoff Carnival.

*It's a Nash tradition!* That's what she says to us every year, and her hopeful expression and wistful tone of voice ropes us all in with an extra side serving of guilt.

I bag a fresh batch of popcorn; the steam rising from the bowl I'm scooping from sends sweat dripping down every part of my body. And I mean *every* part ... my balls are chafing so bad that I want to dunk them in one of those industrial ice machines right now.

"How come Forrest doesn't have to do any of the manual labor?" Fletcher whines.

Forrest answers, speaking in the third person. "Because Forrest is the only one who knows how to operate the credit card app on his cell phone. And Mom trusts me with the money. Now be quiet, you dick. You landed yourself in caramel hell."

Bowen and I shoot each other a somber look. After the incident with Fletcher the other morning, the question of an intervention or rehab is no longer something we have to answer. Time is running out, and we are meeting with Forrest in a few days to plan exactly how we are going to get our brother help.

"Hey, Bowie, did you end up going out with that chick the other night?" Forrest asks, tinkering around with the makeshift cash register he's set up.

My middle brother growls at the use of the nickname, but answers, "If you mean by go out, did I go over to her place and have her moaning my name? Then yes."

I crack up because what else would Bowen have done. He didn't date and was the crudest out of all of us.

Forrest high fives him. "Bro, help me out. The last girl I went out with friend-zoned me after I took her out on three dates and paid!"

"You should pay. Every time." I roll my eyes at him. "And just because you take a girl out doesn't mean she's going to sleep with you."

I felt like his father, lecturing him on treating a woman right.

Forrest shoots me a scowl. "I know that, thanks, *old man*. And I'm not saying she had to, I would never force a woman ..."

"He's just saying he doesn't have enough game to complete the pass." Fletcher chuckles from where he stands stirring the caramel.

"Shut the fuck up!" Forrest yells at his twin.

Bowen walks over to Forrest, rubbing his shoulders and smirking. "Aw, baby bro, do you need tips on how to satisfy a woman?"

"Get away from me." Forrest shrugs him off, and we all laugh.

"When you're ready to learn tips from the master, I'll be here." Bowen flexes his hips suggestively.

"Bowen Nash, behave!" Mom walks into the tent, and we all straighten up like we've just been caught.

"Sorry, Ma." Bowen ducks his head and gets back to work, helping me bag.

We work quietly as the tinker of carnival music sings in the background, and customers come in droves to buy the Nash's caramel corn.

Our family has manned this booth for more than twenty years, and way before my brothers and I were ever the ones doing the work. The Summer Kickoff Carnival is also a Fawn Hill institution, taking place in Bloomsbury Park and running for a whole week. There are rides, games, raffles, food booths set up by all the local restaurants and concerts on the weekend nights.

"Oh, Presley, how nice to see you!" My mom's voice brings me out of my popcorn making concentration.

"Eliza, this smells amazing!"

I turn slowly, trying not to seem too eager. She stands in front of our booth, checking out the operation, and waves slightly when our eyes connect. She's in Daisy Duke jean shorts, scuffed sneakers and a plain white V-neck tee that has me trying to peer down into her cleavage. Her scarlet hair is down in loose curls, and I wonder what it might be like to lick some of our homemade caramel off of her ... lips.

"Hey." I nod.

My brothers all look at me at once, and I want to punch them all in the bicep. *Real subtle, guys.*

"These are my sons. I think you've met Keaton. This is Bowen, and my twins, Forrest and Fletcher." My mom motions to us like we're plates she pulls out for special occasions.

My brothers wave or say hi, but I can see the interest in their eyes. They think she's hot, and I guess I can't blame them. But I still make a sound in the back of my throat without even meaning to, and Bowen's amused eyes hold a question as he looks at me.

"Wow. I didn't realize the hot vet had more hot brothers." She laughs.

Did she just call me hot?

"Oh, I'm sure Keaton didn't tell you how fun the rest of us are. He's the boring one. How are you doing on this fine day?" Fletcher saunters over to the front table in the tent, giving Presley his Cheshire smile.

But before she can answer, Bowen physically turns him back toward the large boiling pots of caramel and shoves the ladle back into his hand.

Her green eyes twinkle with amusement.

"Are you here with anyone?" My mom asks.

"Just my grandma, but she wandered off to talk to the high school vice principal." She shrugs as Bowen hands her a bag of caramel corn, and she tastes a piece. "Wow, this is so good!"

"Well, since you have a free minute, maybe you could accompany Keaton on the Ferris wheel. He was just saying how he wanted to go on it."

Forrest snorts as my stomach drops. My meddling, manipulative mother ... the Ferris wheel of all things. Is she purposely trying to embarrass me?

Presley must catch on to my mother's setup because she smirks at me. "Is that so? Well, you all look kind of busy ..."

"Oh, I insist. He's been working so hard all day, and I'm sure he'd love the company of a beautiful woman such as yourself."

"Mom, stop, she's clearly doing other things and I have to help here."

If I didn't respect and fear my mother so much, I'd wring her neck right now. I should have told her that the woman shot me down not more than a week ago. Being in any kind of confined space after that rejection was going to be humiliating to say the least.

"Okay. Let's go." Presley winks at me as Mom turns her head to beam in my direction.

I blow out a breath. Well, this was going to be awkward.

My brothers wolf whistle as I shed the apron I was wearing and wipe the sweat off my forehead, then leave the booth trailing Presley.

We wait on line for the Ferris wheel without talking, and as the attendant straps the metal bar down over our laps, I'm fully aware of my side pressing right into her side. Sneakers touch sneakers, knees kiss, and her smooth bare arms rub up against mine.

Being this close to her as we ride up, up, up makes me want to do crazy things. The tight control I always have on myself and my life seems to tilt on its axis when this woman is around.

"So, if I ask you out again, are you going to give me a non-answer?"

Presley chuckles. "Look at you, doc, being so direct."

I shrug as our car crests to the top of the wheel again. "I don't really play games, Presley. And you should know, I usually don't date. But I want to date you."

There. It was out there now, and I was being a grown man about this finally. Sure, I was scared shitless, and it was probably a horrible idea to date someone with my past, but from what I'd seen so far, I liked the woman.

Presley's eyes are fixed on mine. "I usually don't date either. I'm not exactly uncomplicated, Keaton."

"No one said I don't have my baggage. But I'm not asking for anything other than a nice night out with you."

Her red mane flutters in the warm night air as she turns

away for a second, looking over the town from our aerial position.

"Okay. One date." She slowly swings her face back to me, a small smile gracing her full lips.

Internally, I high five myself. "It was the caramel corn, wasn't it?"

She throws her head back in a laugh. "Honestly, it was probably your mother. I never want to disappoint that woman, she's so wonderful."

I'd have to thank my mom later for scoring me a date with this beautiful woman. "Would Saturday night work?"

The Ferris wheel brings us down and back up again, stopping while we're about halfway up.

"Tomorrow is Saturday," she deadpans.

I nod. "Yep. I don't want you to change your mind. Plus, I'm not getting any younger. I'll pick you up at seven? You're staying with Hattie, right?"

She looks a little bulldozed, which I kind of like. Presley seems like the kind of girl who usually calls the shots when it comes to her love life, and I want to unbalance her a little. I've never had the urge to be spontaneous or cavalier, but with her, I'm starting to realize that my usual straitlaced rules don't apply.

"Yeah, I'm at Hattie's. How old are you, anyway? And what's your middle name? I should at least know the basics before I go on a date with you. You could be a serial killer."

Her expression is sarcastic, and I grin. "Wouldn't that be a twist? The town veterinarian is actually a real-life Dexter? I'm thirty, and my middle name is William."

Presley nods as if analyzing the two short tidbits of information I've given her. "Hmm, an older man. I don't know how we'll find anything in common with this three-year age gap."

This woman is a ballbuster, and it's interesting to find that her humor is growing on me. I've normally dated quiet, sweet girls.

"Oh, I think we can probably find some common ground." I lean in a little closer and watch her gaze drop to my lips.

She pulls away a little, catching herself.

"Don't worry, Presley. I'm not going to kiss you on this Ferris wheel. You're not a cliché moment kind of girl, that much I can tell. And we haven't even gone on a date yet. You should know I'm a gentleman. A gentleman who doesn't play games. When I kiss you, we'll both be ready for it."

A s usual, there were fourteen discarded outfits on my bed, two hair tools heating on my dresser, and enough makeup to fill a tractor trailer, spilling from the drawers of my nightstand.

And to think, the male on the other end of this date probably took a shower, brushed a piece of hair off his forehead, threw on jeans and a shirt and called it a day.

The absolute madness of being a female and getting ready for a first date was both exciting and extremely awful. My stomach was in knots, I couldn't get my eyeliner to wing the right way, and I was between two outfits that I didn't even really like.

My phone chimed on my rumpled comforter, and I snatched it up.

Ryan: *Wear the blue skirt with the lacy white tank, and a simple, flat sandal. Cute but casual, and if he takes you cow wrangling, you'll have decent footwear.*

Presley: *Cow wrangling? Really?*

I let out a nervous giggle.

Ryan: *shrug emoji* I don't know, I'm just trying to envision what small-town dating looks like.

Presley: We're not living in an eighties western movie. This isn't Footloose. They have Wi-Fi here.

Ryan: Whatever. Go get ready, and text me all the dirty details later. That is, if you're not knocking boots with the sexy vet.

Presley: *eye roll emoji*

There definitely would be no knocking boots with Keaton Nash. For one, I wasn't even sure I wanted to go on this date ...

Okay, I definitely wanted to go on this date. So much so that my palms are sweating as I wait for him on Grandma's front porch. But I also don't want to go at the same time.

In the city, I went on dates. They usually ended in one-night stands, or the guy never calling me again. I didn't form attachments because I was too busy for a boyfriend, and my life is always up in the air as it is, so why add another complication to the mix? There wasn't really a tragic breakup in my past or something like a daddy issue that made me chase bad men. No ... I just had never really wanted a long-term thing, and now that I was older, I almost didn't know *how* to have a boyfriend.

Keaton's charm was silent but deadly; the whole good boy, being direct thing had thrown me for a loop and now here I was, about to get in his car for a night of ... romance? That sounded so cheesy. But he was someone I could actually see myself having a nice time with, so there would be no knocking boots. I was going to be a grown-up about this, even if I had no grown-up job, a bunch of debt, and didn't even own my own car.

Plus, in a town like Fawn Hill, I'm sure half the town would know about my sexcapade before I have my morning coffee tomorrow.

A newer model Toyota truck pulls into Grandma's driveway, and Keaton's long limbs climb out of the driver's seat. He's in a fitted T-shirt and jeans, a much more casual look than I'd seen him in previously. The man still looked gorgeous even in street clothes, with his dirty blond hair slightly gelled back, and his chocolate-colored eyes smiling right along with those full lips. There was some five-o'clock shadow on his jaw, and damn if that didn't make him even more attractive than when he was clean-shaven.

"Hi." He leaned in when he reached my spot on the front steps. "You look amazing."

Those full lips were warm where they pecked quickly at my cheek in greeting. I caught a whiff of his cologne, something earthy with a little citrus that added unexpected spice.

"Thank you. You look ... different." My stupid mouth was failing me already.

Keaton chuckled. "You've seen the boring doctor side. I thought I'd show you how I really am. No wait ... I am kind of a boring doctor."

We both laugh, nervous tinkling filling the air between us.

"But, I thought that tonight, I could show you that I can relax and have fun, too."

My smile is shy. "That sounds good. Should we go?"

He hesitates. "Does Hattie expect me to come in first? Wouldn't want to have your grandmother disapprove of me on the first date."

I roll my eyes. "She said that if you brought her flowers, she'd bash you over the head with them. Told me you were way too good of a catch, and don't screw anything up."

Keaton laughs, and I watch as his biceps, torso, and thighs tense with the motion. It's ... sexy.

And again, I'm reminded of how this man is one giant oxymoron.

"Glad to know she's on my side. Let me get your door."

He walks me to the passenger side and helps me in like a true gentleman. Of all the dates I've been on, this one is off to the best start. Which is sad that it's taken me twenty-seven years to be treated well.

But, I'm hoping, that tonight will change my outlook on a lot of things.

---

"So, should we get the basics out of the way?" Keaton hands the menus to our waiter and smiles at me.

The man wastes no time, which is oddly refreshing.

A candle flickers between us, and I have a feeling this is the nicest restaurant in Fawn Hill. It's clean and smartly decorated, like an old Italian joint with exposed brick and red checkered tablecloths ... but this kind of place wouldn't even make rent in New York City. That was the first snobbish thought that had gone through my head when we walked in. My second was to wonder why he'd brought us somewhere that so many people knew him. Practically every table had waved or greeted Keaton when we walked in, and the owner slash maître d' had hugged him.

"Sure." I nod. "Ask away."

"Well, first, I want you to know something about me. Because I saw your face when we walked in. Sure, I could have taken you to Lancaster, or somewhere farther away where the restaurants are more upscale and we'd be away from the prying eye of nosy townspeople. But ... I want you to really know who I am. Fawn Hill has been my home forever, and I love it here. I've never resented my small-town roots, and my dream was always to take over my father's practice. I enjoy knowing every single person sitting in this restaurant, the intimacy and routine are comfortable to me. Plus, this place has the best chicken parm you'll ever taste, so don't judge the food by the checkered table-cloths." Keaton winks at me. "What I'm trying to say is ... I may not be your usual speed. I know that I'm a 'nice' animal doctor who settled in his hometown. But, I'm glad you gave me a chance."

*Wow*. And that right there is the reason I said yes to this date. Keaton Nash swung between nervous and bumbling, to sure and confident and then back again within days. I never knew what side of him I was going to get. And while his description of his preference of life didn't really match my own, and honestly made me a bit jumpy, I could respect his forwardness.

"I didn't have a face." I can't help the smirk that pulls at my lips.

"You definitely had a smirk. But it's okay, you haven't had the calamari, yet."

"I'll trust your judgment, for now." I raise my eyebrow. "But ... thank you for being honest. It's refreshing. And I don't find it one bit boring. Truthfully, I'm a little jealous of you. You seem like you've always known what you wanted to do, whereas I am an untethered boat washing further and further out into sea."

"Oh, come on, there must be something you're passionate about."

Yoga is the first thing that comes to mind, but I don't tell Keaton. Telling people that you're passionate about exercise and controlling emotions through the form of physical exertion ... well, they just toss it aside as a hobby. If you're passionate about anything creative, someone is going to roll their eyes or doubt you.

"Hmm, I'm just not sure. I'm not one of those people who had the blueprint of their life mapped out in their head since they entered high school."

"Well, it's a good thing opposites attract." Keaton chuckles as a steaming bowl of balsamic calamari is set down between us. "You're looking at the man who recited five-year plans in his head rather than play NASCAR video games."

I spoon some onto my appetizer plate and have to close my eyes after the first bite melts on my tongue. "And a central-Pennsylvania boy would be playing NASCAR games instead of Madden. This is delicious, by the way."

Keaton nods as he chews and reaches for a glass of the red wine he'd ordered. I had the same, but I always found it a little feminine when a man ordered wine.

Honestly, I didn't know how I felt about Keaton Nash yet. With each second, there were more things added to the pro and con sides of my mental list.

"Racing is life, around these parts. There is an old dirt track I should take you too, sometime. Anyway, didn't you mention your love of yoga the other day? Maybe there is something with that you could pursue."

I almost choke on a squid ring. He'd remembered that little detail? "I, uh … yeah, I do like yoga."

"Like I said the other day, Lily at the library could help you get a class going. Might be a great thing for this town."

"Yeah." I nod, still stunned that he recalled the short moment when I'd professed my love for the exercise.

"So, tell me about your family, if we're covering basics first."

An hour later and one stop for dessert, we've extended the date to the local park as the stars make their appearance above. Neither of us suggested ending the night after dinner, and the date has fallen into that dreamy state where we laugh more than talk and dance around each other in the best kind of foreplay possible.

We walk around the lake with ice cream in hand, my stomach already threatening to burst but the mint chip is so good, I can't stop.

"My God, I think I've died and gone to ice cream heaven." I moan as another spoonful hits my tongue.

Beside me, Keaton clears his throat, and when I look up at him, his eyes are molten lava cake. They're perusing my neck and décolletage lazily as he spoons another mouthful of the Oreo fudge swirl past his lips.

My cheeks burn as I look away, because I promised we wouldn't knock boots ... but we've been moving closer and looking longer with each lap we do around the lake in Bloomsbury Park. I have to put some distance, and some words, between us before I mount him over there on that park bench.

As I'd suspected before it had even begun, this was the best date I'd ever been on.

# 10

This is the best date I've ever been on.

I don't know what it is about Presley McDaniel that constantly keeps me interested ... because to be honest, she is the kind of woman I stay far away from. She's flighty and has no plans, where I'm severely type A. She's a city girl with city tastes, except when I took her to our small-town's best eatery, she couldn't get enough of the food. When I ask her about her family, she tells me they aren't really close ... and I'm not sure that's an answer I even comprehend. My family is so up in each other's business that it's hard to tell my brothers apart at times.

Everything about Presley is different from me, and from the girls I usually date.

And yet ... I'm enamored. Every time she talks, I want to hear more. Her sarcasm is refreshing. The way she plays with her vibrant hair nervously when she talks, even though she seems like the most confident woman alive, is such a contradiction.

And the way she's eating that ice cream, making those tiny satisfied noises in the back of her throat ... it's driving me insane. I'm pretty sure I'm looking at her as if I might swallow her whole, and I've fixed my dick trying to tent my pants more times than I can count.

It's been so long since I've been with a woman ... the poor appendage is probably considering just falling off.

I take another bite of Oreo fudge to try to cool down. "Fawn Hill has some of the best creameries in the state surrounding it. We may not have Jamba Juice, but we've got a hell of a ton of good ice cream."

"Which is honestly the better thing. Who cares about diets and smoothies when you can eat this all the time?" Presley laughs, her red locks tousling in the moonlight.

I brought her to my favorite spot by the lake because it's peaceful ... and I didn't want to take her home yet. Heading back toward Hattie's house would mean the date was over, and it was too beautiful of a summer night with too beautiful of a girl to do the gentlemanly thing right now.

At the sake of intruding further, I press something that's been on my mind. "You know, the meadow over this hill would be great for a yoga session. You're lucky you moved to Fawn Hill during the summer ... that's its best season. And I think a morning class would do great among the women in this town."

"Men can do yoga, too." She gives me a judgmental glare.

I hold the hand with a spoon in it up in surrender. "Not what I meant at all ... I was simply saying this might be a nice location."

"Hmm." Presley looks around, and I know she can see it as well.

While she's scoping out the park, her feet accidentally carry her closer in toward me, so that our shoulders bump as we walk. The minute the flesh of our arms connects, there is an instant spark. It's almost visible, like a firefly you weren't quite sure you saw in the darkness. But I hear the sharp intake of breath from

Presley, and when I look down, the moonlight is illuminating the lust in her eyes.

She clears her throat, those green pools trained on mine. "So, can I ask the ever burning question? Why are you still single?"

Internally, I sigh. Because I know what she's doing. She's trying to talk about the least sexy thing possible, the ex-factor, and douse the simmer building between us. We're seconds away from doing something we can't take back, and I have never taken a woman to bed on the first date.

Although Presley McDaniel could be the one to change that.

I force myself to step away from her, to breathe in through my nostrils. I'm so aroused that my balls ache and pulse with each step.

"Oh, you know, just haven't found the right one." I give her the cliché answer.

The last thing I want to do on this first date is get into the real history of my love life. Or the hack job that Katie Flint did to my heart.

Presley taps her chin. "I think you're hiding something."

"And I think someone should mind their own business." It comes out quicker and harsher than I intend, and I cringe the moment it leaves my lips. "I'm so sorry, I didn't mean that."

"So there is some bad history there." Presley nods, not looking at me.

I relent. "There is. But it's not something I like to talk about. So ... I answered the question. Now it's your turn."

"I wouldn't call that an answer, slick. But, I'll play. And it's much the same as your first answer, although it's the truth. I haven't met anyone I really like ... and commitment just isn't on my list of priorities right now."

Her answer burns a hole in both my chest and my gut. I knew she was a free bird, someone who didn't like plans or being tied down. But ... I guess I hadn't realized that a relationship wasn't on her very small to-do list.

"So ... you've never been in a relationship?"

She shrugs. "Not really."

"Right." I zero in on my ice cream, trying to drown out my doubts and fears with dessert.

We walk a little longer, talking about subjects that have the depth of a kiddie pool. The easy conversation returns with the surface-level conversation, and she finishes her mint chip before I'm scraping the bottom of my cup. And then our hands are free, floating by our sides as I contemplate whether I should lace my fingers through hers.

Should I make a move? What is she thinking right now? Is it appropriate to kiss her?

This is why I haven't seen anyone since Katie left two years ago. The pressure, the game ... it's just not me. I don't like it.

We're walking around the side of the lake closest to the parking lot, and our bodies have subconsciously gotten almost shoulder to shoulder again. The buzz of attraction is back, and it seems I can't help but be drawn to this woman. Even if I know she isn't good for me.

I take a deep breath and decide to go for it, gently taking hold of her elbow so that she stops and I can turn to face her.

My other hand goes to her hair, the feature of hers I've been most enthralled with since the first time I saw her. It's soft and thick under my fingers, falling through them like silk. I stare down at her gorgeous, dainty face, which is tipped up to watch the slow descent of my mouth to hers. Her tongue pokes out, wetting her lips, and those clover-green orbs are locked onto my lips.

The heartbeat slamming out erratic rhythms in my chest sends reverberations to every part of my body, and I'm so anxious I could almost jump out of my skin. But at the same time, I'm as calm and steady as I've been my whole life about the path I'm on ... and Presley is the next illogical, improbable step.

Our noses brush, and the current of electricity bending between us could level a city. We're two opposing magnets trying to push through the repelling force and almost succeeding.

"Keaton ..." Presley's voice dashes all of my hope in a nanosecond.

Her hand comes up between us, gently pushing my chest back. "I'm not ready for it."

Shit. I told her next time I asked to kiss her, I'd make sure she was ready. Not only had I not asked her, but I hadn't made sure she was ready. I wasn't lying when I said this woman turned all of my plans to mush.

I straighten, coughing through the embarrassment of yet another rejection from Presley McDaniel, and try my hardest not to adjust the uncomfortable erection now screaming to be released from the zipper on my jeans.

"Honestly, I'm not sure that I even like you, yet."

"Jesus, that's harsh," I choke out, my insulted ego becoming even more injured.

Presley tries to grapple for her thoughts, using her hands to talk. "No, no, that's ... I like you, Keaton. I think you're a good person and you were such a gentleman tonight. But ... we are just very different. For everything you say that I agree with, there is another idea or opinion of yours that I find myself disagreeing with. And I think it's the same for you. I could have let you kiss me, wanted to even, but I'm trying to do this thing where I think before I act. Because that usually gets me in trouble. And you're just so different from me, I'm not sure I've figured out what I think about this, yet."

A beat of silence passes as I digest her words. She's thinking more like I usually would than I have in the last hour.

"I'll get you home, then." My voice is gravelly as I walk just a step ahead of her back to the car.

Let me rephrase my earlier statement. This was the best date I'd ever been on.

And now I highly doubted I was going to get a second one.

# 11

KEATON

My house is a neat split-level two streets over from Main, in a neighborhood near the elementary school.

It's quiet, like the rest of the town, but I like that the cluster of houses had a sidewalk where I could run if I didn't feel like going to the park. When I purchased my house, it was a total gut job. I bought it three years ago ... back when I thought I'd be sharing it with a wife and our children. I renovated the entire place, from bathrooms to bedrooms, and even taught myself how to install a tile backsplash, which was a bitch and I should have hired someone to do it for me.

The house was an investment in the future, and my longtime girlfriend, Katie Flint, Gerry's daughter, had helped me pick almost everything out. Maybe it's why I never felt like this was my home ... that everything in it was matched with the taste of a ghost, a person who no longer lived here.

But I stayed because that's what I did best. For a while, I was the fool waiting for her to come back. And when I realized she wouldn't, I was the fool who stayed here as part of some spiteful plot that she didn't even care about.

"So, when were you going to tell us you had the hots for Hattie McDaniel's granddaughter?" Forrest makes himself right at home, flipping on the television and turning right to the baseball game.

At least he hadn't put on one of his sci-fi shows.

"Or that there was fresh meat in town?" Fletcher asks.

"Don't refer to her like that." He's already pissing me off.

"Damn, I don't think I've ever seen you be this territorial," Bowen muses, going to my pantry to root around for snacks.

"I'm sorry, who told you three you could come over?"

"Or that you took her on a date to Alfiano's?" Forrest continues the line of questioning.

I growl at their intrusion, but I should know better by now. My house was the hangout spot now that none of them wanted to laze around at our childhood home. Too many memories of Dad and too much of Mom's nagging meant they all freeloaded off me and my fridge on the weekends. Saturday and Sundays, I was on call. I'd always go in if an owner needed me, but the office itself was closed for wellness visits or surgeries. What couldn't wait until Monday, I'd take on, but a man needed a few days of relaxation here and there.

"What is this, a firing squad?"

"Yeah, aiming right at your balls if you don't spill the tea." Fletch flops down on my sectional sofa, right on the chaise part.

"Spill the tea?" Bowen smirked ... well, as much as Bowen could smile. It honestly looked like a grimace.

"You're all so stuck in bumfuck that you don't even know the current slang. Spill the tea? Tell us the gossip. Fill us in on the dick down." Fletch says these things like they're not completely ridiculous.

"Okay, where the fuck did you come from?" Forrest throws a chip at his twin.

"Same womb you did, brother."

"Gross, don't even make jokes like that." Bowen shudders. "But, really, Keat, what is going on with you and the redhead?"

I sigh, knowing they'll only keep on with their ridiculousness if I don't answer. "Her name is Presley. She brought her grandmother's dog in after he ate a foreign object—"

"Wait ... Chance is Hattie's dog, right? Wait a fucking minute, is this the dog who ate the lace underwear?" Forrest's eyes light with glee.

I now regret telling them any story from my job, even if they looked at me with something other than bored, forced interest for half a second.

Pointing my finger at my brother, I continue, "I'm not answering that. Anyway, I saw her around town ... and I asked her out."

"First girl you've looked at enough to do something about since Katie," Bowen says quietly.

I know that he knows it's not just some one-off thing for me to ask a woman out on a date.

"So ... how'd it go? You are tighter than the broad—"

"Do not finish that sentence!" I yell at Fletcher. "It ... let's just say there probably won't be a second date."

Forrest stops flipping through channels and Bowen stops mid-bite of his chip and salsa. And then all three of my brothers say at the same time,

"The sex was bad, wasn't it?"

The male ego of this conversation could punch a hole through concrete. "We didn't have sex."

"Well, there is your first problem." Fletcher ticks off a finger.

"I agree." Forrest nods.

"As if I'd take the first woman I've dated in two years to bed on the first night." I roll my eyes.

Bowen grins sheepishly. "Honestly, Keat, and I know you ... but I agree with them. If anyone needs to get off, it's you."

"Thanks, brother." I glare at him.

"Why aren't you going out again?" Forrest asks.

I pick at the sweatshirt I have on, trying not to make eye contact. "She rejected my kiss."

"I'm sorry, what was that? You're mumbling." Fletcher moves closer to me.

Sighing, I raise my voice. "She rejected my kiss."

My youngest brother begins to howl with laughter while Forrest gives me a sympathetic look and Bowen just pats me on the shoulder where he sits on my other side.

"Tough break, man. But she's super-hot. Way out of your league." Forrest shrugs as if I know this about myself.

"Gee, thanks, guys. Way to make a guy feel good about himself."

Bowen looks thoughtful. "Hmm, I don't think she's out of his league. Sure, she's gorgeous and Keat's just average, but he's a doctor. Which gives him bonus points. Maybe ask her out again … I mean, you must like her if you asked the first time."

Glancing at him, I know what he's trying to do. The same thing my middle brother has been attempting since Katie left. Help me to move on.

"The worst she could say is no … again." Fletcher starts cracking up and I whip the pillow behind my back out and smack him in the face.

"Enough ragging on big brother. Or I'll kick you all the fuck out of my house."

There, that'll teach them to disrespect their elders.

Fletcher and Forrest giggle together, and Bowen pretends not to smile as he shoves more chips in his mouth.

# 12

My hands are sweating, and I wipe them down my black mesh-paneled leggings.

I mean, I'm usually sweating during a yoga class, but this is ridiculous. Good thing I wore black workout pants today because if they were any lighter of a color, it would look like I peed my pants.

With five minutes to go before my first yoga class hosted by the Fawn Hill library begins, there are only two other women here. And neither of them have yoga mats.

Good thing I'd invested in some cheap ones on Amazon and dragged them along to Bloomsbury Park. Lily, the librarian and all-around perfectionist of Fawn Hill, had helped me so much when I'd gone to her with the idea of doing a weekly yoga class in the park on Friday mornings. She printed up the flyers, sent out an email newsletter, and it helped that she knew literally everyone in town and was shoving the event down their throats. I'd been responsible for coming up with the sequence we'd move through during our practice, providing materials like mats and water, and introducing the naïve town of Fawn Hill to my favorite exercise of both the body and mind.

To say I was nervous would be an understatement. This was the first real initiative I'd taken in my life, besides moving to Fawn Hill to help Grandma with the shop. I wanted it to be successful, especially because I love the practice of yoga so much. Hopefully, the townspeople will like it just as much, and I could continue these little pop-up workouts. The thought of having something of my own, that I was really proud of, was surprisingly great motivation.

And the person who had encouraged me, twice, to do it? Keaton Nash.

Just thinking about Dr. Tall, Dark, and Distracting was ... well, *distracting*. I blushed to myself, my stomach fluttered and I almost raised my fingertips to my lips. But then I realized I'd probably look like a crazy person to these two strangers waiting for class to start, and I stopped myself.

But that didn't mean I wasn't thinking about that almost kiss. It felt funny to even call it that because I'd stopped it. There was no doubt that if he'd kissed me, Keaton would probably go down as the best set of lips to ever dance with mine. But I'd pushed him away after our conversations mixed my head up to the point of frustration. And even after I'd said no to a kiss, he still waited at the bottom of the front steps to see that I made it inside and locked the door. I'd be lying if I said it wasn't the best, and most confusing, date I'd ever been on.

"Did someone say yoga?" Lily walks over the hill, yoga mat in hand, and down into the flat space I'd designated for today's class.

"Lily, thanks for coming." I smile at her, happy to have a familiar face here.

She unrolled her mat, her petite, tight body envious. I had been a little stunned to find the young, pretty brunette behind the librarian's desk when I'd gone to inquire about starting a class. Lily was bubbly, organized, friendly and just about the complete opposite of what you thought of when you pictured a stuffy, old librarian. I understood why she had the job though because, in Fawn Hill, it was much more than just alphabetizing books. She was the cornerstone of community events, knew all the right people for anything you might be looking for, and worked extremely closely with the local schools.

"Of course! Did you think I was going to miss this town's first opportunity at a gym? Hell, I'm hoping you spin this into a place I can actually come to sweat because lord knows I could use the outlet." She was already bouncing on the balls of her sneakers.

"Well, first comes first, take your shoes off. We do yoga barefoot." I chuckle at her enthusiasm.

The other two women, who look to be in their thirties, follow suit. I sigh, checking my watch again, and see that there is only two minutes before the nine a.m. class is supposed to begin. I guess this is going to be it and resign myself to the fact that I didn't pull this off.

Just as I take my place in front of them, with my heels meeting the edge of my turquoise mat, I hear a gaggle of laughter coming down the hill from the parking lot. Looking up, there are at least twenty women making their way to us.

A tall blond with perfect curls and long, slim arms, waves at us. "So sorry! We were in the wrong part of the park! So glad we found you in time."

I hope my mouth isn't hanging open, and I see Lily wink at me. "Told you, girl. This town will eat a yoga class up."

The blonde walks up and grabs Lily into a hug and a kiss, and it'c clear these women know each other well.

"Oh, Lily is so right, we have been waiting forever for this. The mom crowd is going to go nuts for this. I'm Penelope, by the way."

Swallowing, I attempt to remain cool and wave at all of my newcomers, including their clear leader, Penny. "Welcome, everyone! If you could roll out your mats and remove your shoes, we'll get going here in just a minute. There are coolers of water over there if you need a drink during our practice, and I ask that we try to remain as quiet as possible while we go through our sequences, no matter how many of us fall over, including me!"

That gets some laughs, and two minutes after that, I'm walking them through their first down dog.

Forty minutes later, we're finishing up, lying on our mats in the middle of the park on a gorgeous summer morning, the blue sky smiling down on us. I lie on my mat, looking up at the clouds, with a huge grin plastered on my face.

*I did it. I actually freaking did it.*

Hosting a yoga class in the park of the smallest town I've ever stepped foot in might not sound like the biggest accomplishment, but for me, it is. I followed through with something, and it went off without much of a hitch. I'd count this as a success, and honestly, I don't think it's getting ahead of myself to say this will be a continuous thing. For the first time in a long time, I'm truly proud of myself.

Penelope sits up, her white leggings and blush pink tank top super trendy. "Well, Presley ... can we do it again tomorrow? I feel so relaxed! Who knew a mom of three could be this de-stressed?"

When she mentions the word mom, I startle a little. This woman looks younger than me, and the six-pack you can practically see through her shirt certainly did not hold children.

Most of the women nod in unison with her, and Lily stands up. "I just want to thank Presley for hosting our first yoga class, can we give her a round of applause?"

I'm showered with almost twenty-five women clapping for my success. I honestly have to choke back tears, and it's not the first time in the last hour that I've almost cried out of joy.

"You can sign up for her next class using the form on the library website, and since this was a pilot class, it was free. But from now on, each session will be five dollars, with two of those going to the library and three going to our wonderful teacher."

Speechless. I'm fucking speechless at what Lily just announced.

So Lily speaks for me as everyone rolls up their mats and hang around to chat or head to their cars. "Thank you, ladies! See you next week!"

After the last of the women clear out, I walk to Lily with the half-empty water cooler in my arms.

"I don't even know what to say. You didn't have to announce the price increase ... from zero dollars." I laugh. "I didn't need any money for this, I'm happy to do it for free. Honestly, I love yoga and this was really fun."

"But you *should* get paid for it, and don't let those women fool you. They can afford it. You should turn this into something, Presley. You're a very good teacher."

"You're kind of pushy, huh?"

She smiles sneakily. "But in a friendly way, don't you think?"

"Yeah, I'll give you that." I chuckle as we turn to walk to our cars.

"Which is why you're going to join me for a celebratory cup of coffee at Fawn Hill Java."

"That's not a request, is it?"

"Just a friendly little demand." She smirks.

"All right, I'll follow you there."

"Did you catch the game last night?"

I ask Bowen this as if he's actually going to elaborate on this conversation in more than a few words.

"Yeah. Shit pitching." My brother drains his first cup of coffee and motions for Dylan, one of the regular employees at Java, to come refill his cup.

Well, at least he expressed a thought to continue on. "Yeah, Pittsburgh really needs to pull some kids out of their farm system or trade or something, or we're going to miss the playoffs again this year."

Bowen grunts, which officially ends the conversation. I love my brother, but he's not great company. He has his demons, that I know, but they've turned him into a shell of his former self.

And my fucking God, sometimes irony is a cold bitch. Because at the exact moment I begin to think about my brother's demons, the biggest one walks right through the door of the town coffee shop.

On the heels of my current crush.

"Shit." Bowen spots Lily at the same time I do.

"It's fine, Bow. We can all coexist, you've seen her before.

We're enjoying our coffee. I'm sure they'll leave soon." I wish I could inject my brother with Xanax.

He's rubbing his clavicle in the same spot he broke it in three places all those years ago, and my stomach clenches for him. The shit he's been through, especially where it comes to Lily, is heavy.

I'm not even worried about my heart, even though it's badly bruised. Presley smiles from where she and Lily have just picked up their coffees from the other end of the counter. Now that we've seen each other, we can't just ignore it. She smiles at me, and I can see the bad end to our date the other night written all over her face.

To her, this is an awkward run in. But for my brother and Lily, and me who knew their past, this was a hundred levels worse than Presley and I's interaction was going to be.

"Hey." Presley smiles, and I can't help but let my eyes roam over her body.

Goddamn, did she have to be so attractive?

"Hey, you look great. How did class go?" It was a chore to keep my tongue from lolling out of my mouth.

What is it about yoga pants that made everything on a woman sexier? Especially Presley.

It was also a chore to keep my wounded pride from rearing its ugly head. We hadn't spoken since our date ended in disaster last weekend, and I know she's just over here for a pity hello. And even though she rejected me, and not for the first time, I still want to show my support. Presley is bright and smart, even in the short time I've known her I've figured that out. I've also figured out that she downplays that, and she seems to make herself smaller. I'm not sure why, and I'm not sure I'll ever find out since she admitted to not knowing if she really likes me.

*Ouch.* That still burns.

"Yuck, I'm all gross. But it went well, we had a great turnout.

And there is going to be a next time so that's something." Her smile reveals just how psyched she is about this even if she was trying to downplay it.

"She did a great job," Lily added, sneaking a glance at Bowen.

My brother was actively trying not to spaz out like a crazy person and sprint out of the coffee shop, I could tell by his posture and the way his foot was hammering into the floor.

"You all must know each other, right? Everyone in this town knows each other." Presley laughs innocently.

As much as I want to see her, despite her rejection, I wish she wasn't here right now. Because it would mean Bowen wouldn't have to face the girl whose heart he crushed to smithereens, and who did the same to him.

"You could say we know each other." Bowen's voice is deadly calm, and it has the hairs on the back of my neck standing at attention.

Lily looks like she's about to cry, and I don't need Bowen doing something stupid. He's got his life in order, he doesn't need one mistake to throw it off track.

I get up abruptly, because I can feel the tension about to reach a boiling point. "We should go. You ladies enjoy your coffee. Presley, I'll ... see you later."

*What?* God, that was a stupid thing to say.

Presley looks surprised, and I watch as Lily lets out a long, relieved breath. Bowen exits before I can even move from the table, and at the last second, my hand finds hers and squeezes.

The smile that spreads her lips is genuine, and a flutter of hope passes through my chest. Maybe, just maybe, I have one more chance with this woman.

# 14

"What was that all about?"

I'm genuinely confused at what just went down between Keaton, his brother, and Lily.

We sit at their recently vacated table and I take a long pull from the latte I ordered. The sweet vanilla and creamy milk give me energy I wasn't aware I needed, and suddenly I'm so hungry I don't know how I lasted so long without food. I put down the coffee and dig into my egg sandwich, sighing as the first bite hits my tongue.

"We might need to bring snacks to yoga next time." Lily smiles at my cavewoman antics, but I still see the sadness lingering in her big blue orbs.

"Do you want to talk about Bowen?" I can be a bit nosy.

She blinks at me. "No one ever just comes out and asks me that in this town. It's actually kind of refreshing ... both that you know nothing about our history but also are here if I really want to talk about it."

And now I'm super curious what the heck happened between those two, because if the whole town knows ... it must be pretty bad. But Lily and I are just forming a friendship, and I don't want to pry.

"Listen, I'm not going to make you tell me if you don't want to, but I'm just letting you know I'm here for you." I pat her hand.

Look at me, the city girl turning into a country bumpkin ... I'm touching strangers and offering up shoulders to lean on. Who am I? In the months since moving to Fawn Hill, I've asked myself that question more times than I can count.

And I'm kind of surprised that I feel the most like *myself*, whoever that is, since I've been here. The small-town life suits me more than I ever thought it would.

"Bowen and I were high school sweethearts. I don't know how much you know about the Nash brothers ... but Bowen was much like Fletcher when we were in high school. Dangerous, rambunctious, a risk-taker. We were young and in love and felt invincible. And it led to ... a horrible accident. We were involved in a car accident and both almost died. It ... ruined both of our lives in several ways."

She looks so upset that I think she might cry, and I move to sling an arm around her shoulder and hug her close.

"I am so sorry, Lily."

Blowing out a shaky breath, she nods a thank you at my comfort. "The worst part is, it ruined our relationship. I thought I was going to marry Bowen, we might have been in high school but I knew that I knew. Since the night of the accident, he won't speak to me. Won't even look at me ... but I still love him."

This last sentence is whispered, and I see the tear trail down her olive-skinned cheek. Her pain is palpable, and in that moment, I wish I could take it away.

Lily clears her throat. "Jeez, I didn't mean to unload my life story on you." She wipes a tear and moves out of my embrace, so

I swing my chair back around to the other side of the table. "How do you know Keaton, anyway?"

It's my turn to grin uncomfortably and have nerves wrack my body. "We, uh ... we went on a date."

Her blue eyes go wide. "You? You went on a date with Keaton Nash?"

I'm slightly offended at the tone of her question. "Yes, me. Why, am I totally out of his league?"

"No, if anything, he's out of yours. It's just that Keaton doesn't date, not since his ex, Katie, left him two years ago."

I tap the side of my coffee cup. "Ah, the dreaded baggage. I think I hit a nerve when I asked about that on our date last weekend."

Lily makes a sympathetic face. "Putting aside my association with the Nash brothers ... I'll just say that Keaton is an absolute sweetheart. He's down-to-earth, clearly you can see how attractive he is, and he's got a great gig going here taking over his father's practice. But, about two years ago, things really went south for him. He had been dating Katie, who grew up here too, for a long time. They were Fawn Hill's young golden couple; they bought a house together, she brought him bagged lunches to the office, and it was just kind of a known fact that they'd get married and give birth to the next generation of Fawn Hill's popular kids. But then, one day, she just packed up and left. Broke his heart, from the gossip spewed around town. And then, about three weeks after she left, his father passed away. It was a horrible, horrible time. I don't know if he's ever quite recovered."

This new information changes the light I see Keaton Nash in. From first glance, I thought he was a hot animal doctor. After talking on different occasions, I know he's a small-town boy with a big heart and speaks honestly. But with this new download from Lily? I get a glimpse of the hurt lingering around Keaton Nash.

Thinking about it now, his whole aura is tinged with sadness. He might not show it, but it's there, buried under the surface. I'd nicked it once, and he'd snapped at me for it. Having the woman you thought you'd spend the rest of your life with up and leave you? That changed a person. It said to me that Keaton wasn't as put together as he tried to appear, that he had demons and heartbreak lurking close by.

But losing your father, the man who groomed you for your career, pass away shortly after that? It altered a person. Tragedy would always warp the soul and take just a little piece of humanity away from the body.

"Wow, I ... I had no idea."

Lily tilts her head. "No, you wouldn't, would you? No outsider would. That's the thing about living here ... everyone knows your secrets. Maybe Keaton thought you could be his clean slate."

And I'd dirtied his slate right back up again with my refusals. I'd basically told him that I thought he was too ... small for me. Too pure. Too *good*.

I had a feeling, now, that I knew very little about the man.

"Maybe he was." I pondered, looking out the cafe window and across the street at his office.

# 15

A pparently, Fawn Hill moms and twenty-somethings can spread news faster than a viral meme.

Within three days, my next yoga class was the talk of the town, and Lily had booked my next Friday class to the max. She'd had so much interest, that she'd asked if I would be open to hosting a Saturday morning class as well. Both paid for by the attendees, and I had, hopefully, found myself a new gig.

I thought life in rural Pennsylvania was going to be slow and boring, but between learning the ropes at the bookshop and planning my weekly yoga classes, I was pretty damn busy.

In New York, I'd worked double waitressing shifts and taught five yoga classes a week. I was burnt out all the time, rarely went out with friends, and had zero direction. When I was in it, I thought I was happy. That I was hustling, grinding as a twenty-something and living my life my own way. I would never be the professional career person that my brother and sister were. I reveled in the fact that I was the family's black sheep. It was my spiteful cross that I bared and I wore my scarlet letter proudly.

But now, I wondered, for what? I wasn't working toward anything. If I had to be honest, I was miserable.

Pulling out clothes now, in preparation for tomorrow, my Saturday morning class, I can't seem to find my favorite sports bra. Pale pink, crisscrossing straps in the back, keeps my girls in place and supported.

"Where the hell ..." I muse as I rifle through drawers.

And then I hear it. The burp from the other side of my bed. Rounding the queen frame, I look down.

Right into the guilty face of Chance, my grandmother's bad, meddling dog.

"You have got to be kidding me." Both hands fly to my hips as if giving this creature attitude will force my bra to magically appear from his stomach.

Shit. Well, I have other bras, but the dog should probably get checked out.

I walk down the stairs of my grandmother's house. It's a two-story colonial with three bedrooms. The design is old, but she keeps it neat, and there is a certain charm about living in a home with so much history and character. There is even one of those old ironing boards slash desks that flips down from a wall in the kitchen.

When I find my grandma, she is sitting in the recliner she's laid claim to, no one else can sit there, watching a rerun of *The Golden Girls*.

"Your stupid dog ate another piece of my clothing," I whine.

Her eyes flick up. "Another thong? That dog is such a horn-ball. You'd think I never cut off his balls."

Gross. "No, he ate ... one of my sports bras this time."

She chuckles. "Ah, the matching set. At least he knows what to pair things with. Well, call the vet."

Her finger hits the volume button on the remote, turning it up a few notches.

"Can't you call? It's your dog, and I took him last time."

Grandma turns to me, her green eyes full of sass. "I'm not the one who can't keep my room clean. Don't blame this all on the dog. Plus, aren't you knocking boots with Dr. Nash? I'm sure he'd take much more kindly to an after-hours call from you than he would from me."

"Why does everyone assume we're knocking boots?" I throw my hands up. Goddamn this town and its rumor mill. "We're not, by the way. Nor are we seeing each other. So can't you just call him?"

This time, she doesn't even spare me a glance. "No can do, darlin'. Your bra, your mess. Call the man. And go out with him again, you're wasting a perfectly handsome face on your commitment issues."

Heated, embarrassed blood fills my cheeks. How dare she pinpoint the exact thing I'm afraid of and call me out for it? It sucks having a mirror shoved in your face.

"I don't have his phone number." I throw out another reason.

"It's on the notepad by the fridge, along with all the other emergency numbers. You should probably learn those. And take Chance out to pee before you put him in the car, would you?"

It's a miracle steam isn't billowing from my ears as I pull out my cell phone on the way to the kitchen. Who actually kept a pad by their fridge anymore?

The number listed is for the veterinary office on Main Street, and I know it has to be closed at eight p.m. But I call anyway, listening to the phone ring over and over. Then the call clicks over and the ringing sounds different, and I'm surprised when someone picks up.

"Hello, this is Dr. Nash."

That crisp, manly, good-natured voice has a small smile spreading across my lips. Of course, all the after-hour calls are transferred directly to him.

"Hi, Keaton, it's Presley." I shuffle my feet nervously. Thank God no one can see me.

A beat of silence. "Presley? Sorry, I answered like a stuffy doctor, I thought this was my work line transferring over."

"It is, I'm calling because Chance ate something. Again. I wanted to see what you thought I should do?"

A gruff chuckle. "God, that dog is something else. Has he eaten tonight? Gone to the bathroom?"

I try to think. "Um, well he ate dinner before he ate my clothing. And I haven't tried to take him out yet ..."

As I finish the tail end of filling Keaton in, Chance walks into the kitchen and starts making gagging noises.

"Oh, crap. Now he's making those horrible dog vomit noises." The sound makes my skin crawl. It's akin to nails on a chalkboard.

Keaton sighs, and I can hear him moving or shuffling on the other end. "Better bring him in. Can you meet me at my office in fifteen minutes?"

"Yes. I'm sorry to have to make you come in after-hours." I genuinely feel bad for this dog's crap timing.

"Don't worry, it's all part of the job," he responds, hanging up after a goodbye.

A tiny pang of wishing moves through me.

Part of me kind of wished he were doing this because it wasn't part of his job. And how twisted is that?

Twenty-five minutes later, and my arm is fist deep in Chance's rectum again.

The things you think you'll never say ... and then you become a vet.

"I don't feel anything yet, no tangling or irregularities." Removing my hand, I snap off my glove and throw it in the trash.

Being on-call all the time is pretty much part of the job description. I'm the only veterinarian in town, and in most of the rural surrounding towns. I'd say I see an animal after I close up shop about three out of the seven days of the week. I don't mind really ... what else am I doing? I'm a bachelor who eats mostly frozen microwave meals and watches whatever sports game is on television that night.

Moving around Chance, who lies lazily on the table in front of me, I feel his abdomen and throat. They both feel fine, no obstructions or bloating.

"Just keep an eye on him and monitor his bowel movements. You should see most of the ... I'm sorry what did he eat, again?"

Presley flushes a deep pink, and I'm reminded of the first day she walked into my practice. "He ate one of my sports bras."

I run a hand through my hair, blowing out a smiling breath. "He's a randy bastard, isn't he?"

"That he is." She laughs.

It's ... strange having her here. In my office, just the two of us, an exam room light the only thing burning the midnight oil. Well, I guess we have Chance the undergarment eating dog here as well, but he's about ready for bed. Whereas, all I can do is try to look anywhere but at the beautiful vixen standing on the other side of the table.

"Just monitor him for the next few days, but he should be fine. And try to keep him gated off until Hattie takes my advice on those training courses. One of these times, he's really going to hurt himself."

She nods, looking guilty. "I'm a bit of a slob, so I guess tidying up is part of his treatment, too. Thank you again for coming in for this. I really apologize if we interrupted your night."

My laugh is a quick hoot. "If by my night you meant a Hungry Man on the couch with the baseball game on in the background, then yeah, you ruined a lot. I'm not exactly the one painting the town red if you hadn't noticed."

Presley toys with the cardigan she has on, and I wonder if she's hot in it. The thought of stripping her out of it has my blood heating. Jeez, maybe my brothers are right. It's been a *long* time for me.

"Something I admire about you is your honesty, Keaton." The words out of her mouth surprise me.

"Okay? Thanks?" I'm not sure if she's trying to pad my wounded ego from what happened between us.

She toys with the hem of her jean shorts, which only draws my eyes to those mile-long legs. "Full disclosure, because I'm trying to be a better person since moving here, Lily told me a little bit about your past."

My first reaction is to move away from her, which I do. I step back, almost in self-preservation. I don't need to talk about this, especially to a woman I'm crushing on that also rejected me.

Presley holds her hands up. "No, I'm sorry, I didn't mean for that to come off as ... like I was prying. Lily simply wanted to know how we knew each other, and, again, in all honesty, I *wanted* to know more about you. You intrigue me, Keaton. And if I'm being completely up front ... I'm attracted to you."

This has my head whipping straight forward, eyes pinned on her. "Could have fooled me."

My tone is both sarcastic and accusatory, so unlike my usual demeanor. But, Presley, she brings something out in me.

She shrugs. "Yeah, I've been hot and cold. Blame it on my complete life upheaval and the fact that the draw you have scares the crap out of me."

*I* scare *her*? What alternate universe had I stepped into?

"This has got to be some kind of joke." I run my hands over my face, laughing. "Do you even know how intimidating you are? You're this gorgeous, big city, worldly gypsy who is instantly lovable but cold and aloof at the same time. I'm a small-town vet with a mortgage. I'm not even a real doctor, which would make me a little more interesting."

"Hey, don't talk about Keaton Nash that way." She scowls at me, teasing. "The only thing you're highlighting is how different we are, which I've never had a problem seeing. But, talking to Lily, it opened my eyes to the side of you I wasn't aware of. All of that shine has some grit underneath. Obviously, I don't wish bad upon you ... but, this sounds so bad. I thought you were just this perfect, goody-two shoes. I misjudged you, and I realize that's something I do often with a lot of people. I apologize. When you're ready to tell me, I'd like to hear more about what makes you, well, *you*."

Her confession both relieves me and puts me on edge. Knowing that she judged me on our initial meeting is hard to swallow. But, I'm almost glad Lily outed my past, because I don't know how forthcoming, or when, I would have been with Presley. I won't lie, I put on the good boy front to protect myself. Knowing she wants to hear about Katie, about my father ... that unnerves me.

"I don't open up about that much." My voice has a warning tone.

Presley's eyes weigh my change in demeanor, and she moves toward me across the exam room.

"I understand that. There are things I don't talk about much."

Chance snorts where he lies on the table, and we both chuckle at how much we're boring him. Presley's on the same side of the room as I am now, and my fingertips spark with the need to reach out and touch her. We're alone, the only two people in this whole building, and it's too tempting.

She may have shot me down more times than I'd like to count, but that mysterious pull is still there.

"And there are things I do. Stupid things." Presley inches closer.

Her perfume, a sweet vanilla with a zing of citrus, tickles my nose. Her steps are silent as she tiptoes toward me, and all I can do is stand here uselessly. The nerdy high school boy takes over my body, and I just can't believe that this beautiful creature is looking at me the way she's looking at me.

"Are you going to kiss me, Keaton?" She blinks up, her expression vulnerable.

I have to lick my lips to get the words out, my throat is so dry. "I don't know. Last time, you didn't want me to."

Presley is so close now that the soft fabric of her T-shirt brushes against mine. The tiny bit of friction shoots straight to my loins.

"But now, I'm ready."

Those two words are all I have to hear to step into her space, slide my hands into her hair, and gently tilt her head up and to the side so that I have the best angle on those full, peachy lips.

Presley lets out a soft sigh right before I lower my mouth and kiss her.

Slow and searching, I press my lips to hers, leading this dance of ours. Her eyes flutter shut a moment before mine do, and then my four other senses are left to their own devices. She presses up against me, the fabric between us suddenly suffocating. Our mouths move in tandem, a caress here, a nip there, a lick to explore.

One hand strokes her silky locks and the other moves down to her jaw, tipping it up to give me better access. I push my tongue in, lapping at hers. The intimacy is seductive and I'm so turned on that I don't even think before removing my hand from her hair and bringing it to her hip. I grind against her, holding her steady so she can feel how hard she's making me. It's painful, this arousal, and the need to touch more, see more of her, is sharp in the air.

We kiss like time has stood still, deep and longing as if this is the air we've always been meant to breathe but haven't swallowed it until right this moment. And I know now that I've never really a kissed a woman, not until Presley. All of those years, I thought I'd been happy.

How could I have ever settled for that?

There is that saying, "where have you been all my life?" Right now, it had never been truer.

Our kiss comes to an abrupt halt when Chance rouses from his slumber and makes a truly horrific gagging noise.

My forehead sinks into Presley's shoulder as we both chuckle at our cockblock culprit.

"Do you want to ... go somewhere?" She's all breathy and her lashes kiss her cheeks as her eyes stay closed.

As much as I'd like to take her back to my place and remedy the dry spell my brothers keep making fun of me for ... those things I can't talk about are holding me back. I've never been the type to move fast, and with how my interactions with Presley have gone so far, I want to test the waters more.

"Well, I'm officially off the clock. So how about a drink?"

Green jewels under hooded eyelids assess me. "The bar across the street?"

Fuck. I'd forgotten for a second. That Fawn Hill had only one bar, and that said bar was owned by my ex-girlfriend's father. Not only did I not want to see him, but no way did I want him to know I was seeing someone. Even if his daughter cared nothing about me anymore.

Walking out of the exam room and to my office, I open the bottom drawer of my desk. Presley comes in a minute later, confusion written all over her face.

I hold up a bottle of Maker's Mark. "I have a better idea."

"Well, Dr. Nash, how adventurous of you."

I look up at the water tower in front of us, and the butterflies that have taken up residence in my gut flutter madly. When he said he had something else in mind, I didn't imagine it would be so ...

*Cool.*

This is exactly the kind of spontaneous that speaks to my soul, and the fact that the man who just kissed the pants off me has brought us here is exciting.

I'm tempted to stay down here just to kiss him more. Climbing will delay us, and, my lord, I've delayed too much with this man for too long. If I'd known Keaton Nash could kiss that way, that it would be so toe-curlingly amazing ... I would have done it sooner.

My fingers itch to touch my lips or to dive back into his hair. Ever since we left his office, I've had to physically restrain myself from jumping him. The only thing that stopped me from asking him to come up to my bedroom when we dropped Chance off at home was my grandmother sleeping in the next room.

But he'd been the one to suggest this mystery rendezvous,

instead of going to the town bar. Or a mattress. I had to appreciate that. He's taking things slow, which was great because lord knew I was weak enough to have sex with him right there in his exam room. At least one of us was trying to control ourselves. And I also kind of preferred not to air our connection yet. Since we'd gone to dinner, random people would stop me on the street and ask how Keaton and I were doing.

The residents of Fawn Hill were nosy as shit, and I wanted to stay in the bliss bubble for a while.

"Always wanted to do this ... but was too chickenshit. Being with you makes me feel like I can be a badass even if I'm home before midnight." He chuckles.

I bring out the crazy in him ... I'm not sure if that's a good or a bad thing. "Let's go up."

Keaton follows me up the rickety, long ladder. It didn't look like much of a climb from the bottom, but as I reach the top and shimmy onto the platform, I gulp as my eyes search the darkness for the ground.

"Didn't think it would be such a long fall." The railing suddenly seems very unsafe.

"Don't tell me you're afraid of heights. You come from the city with the tallest buildings in the country."

Keaton finds my hand and when his fingers lace through mine, I feel marginally better. "Those buildings also have air-conditioning and Starbucks on the middle level cafe floor. This is completely different."

"But beautiful." Keaton points up.

And I'm met with the biggest tapestry of stars I've ever seen. It's like they all got together and knitted a quilt of bursting light in the sky.

"And if you still don't feel steady, how about a drink?" I can make out his grin in the dark.

He unscrews the bottle and holds it to his lips, his head

tipping back to invite the liquor. I think he's going to swallow and hand me the bottle, but he bypasses that completely and goes straight for my mouth.

This kiss is more insistent, spicy with the liquor burning between our tongues. I'm intoxicated, and it has nothing to do with the alcohol sliding down my throat. Keaton goes to pull back, but I keep a tight hold to his face, the scruff of his well past five-o'clock shadow scraping against my palms. He chuckles into my mouth, a hoarse, manly sound that has me feasting on his lips.

Arousal sneaks over me slowly, like an all-consuming fog, wrapping its luscious tendrils around my arms, legs, belly, and down to my core. I have to lean against Keaton for support, my legs are threatening to liquefy. The spark that has started inside me, where that hot nub of sensation burns, is begging to be satisfied.

"I feel like a teenager, sneaking out to meet a boy." I break off our make-out session and giggle.

I'm too wound up already ... and the humid summer night air is doing nothing to help. If I don't put the brakes on, we're going to be doing a lot racier things than I was doing as a seventeen-year-old.

"Well, I have already seen your underwear, and bra might I add, so I think we're a little more advanced than teenagers."

"I don't know what you were doing as a teenager, but nowadays, I'm pretty sure second base is akin to being prude. Get with it, old man."

Keaton squeezes my hip, tickling me until I squirm away. "I might be thirty, but my old ass just climbed all the way up here and I didn't even break a sweat. Plus, I *was* a total prude back then. The typical nerdy, advanced math kind of teenager."

"I find that hard to believe." I roll my eyes. "Look at you.

You've got popular jock written all over you, even if you did like math."

"I was better at science." He shrugs with a teasing smirk. "But I did play baseball."

My finger stabs gently at his firm chest. "See? I knew it."

"What were you like in high school?" He takes another sip out of the bottle.

How do you tell the man you have a huge crush on that you were the loner in high school? The party girl who was more likely to be Ally Sheedy than Molly Ringwald.

"I had purple hair in high school. Cut class a lot to weave dream catchers and smoke. You think I'm a hippie now, you should have seen me back then. Lord, I thought I was so cool."

Even I have to laugh at the moronic way I used to act.

"Purple hair, huh? I like the red better." Keaton leans back in, resuming our kiss.

He's pressed against me, so I feel it when his phone vibrates.

"Ah, hold on one second, I'm sorry." He smiles apologetically and digs his phone out. "Shit ..."

Keaton looks down at his phone and runs a shaky hand through his hair. With his face lit up by the screen, I watch as anger slowly replaces the lust I just put there.

I wonder what he just read, and if it's something he is going to try to hide.

"It's my brother, the youngest one, Fletcher. He's ... he has some problems. My brother Bowen, the one you met, needs my help. I'm so sorry, but I have to go."

My heart believes him and stops itself in its tracks from jumping to too many conclusions. "Do you want me to come with you?"

He doesn't even look at me as he makes his way over to the ladder. "No, sorry. This family stuff ... it's complicated. I'll drop you at home, it's on my way."

Welp, guess that's the end of our night. Responsibility and adulthood call, and Keaton is the first to jump to attention.

And even though I'm not going to be able to sleep thinking of the kissing, the burn of his refusal to let me into his life stings more than I thought it would.

# 18

A flash of pain radiates down my spine, but I'm semi-conscious and want to turn it off.

Sleep. I need more sleep.

Except, a second later, more pain news at my back, and I'm forced to open my eyes and sit up. I look around to find that I passed out on Bowen's couch, so it's no wonder my back feels like it's got about three hundred Charlie horses cramping it up. Thirty-year-old bodies cannot sleep on unsupported sectionals or climb water tower ladders without consequences the next day.

Christ, last night was a clusterfuck. After making out with Presley on the town water tower, which was definitely the highlight of the night, I'd rushed off to help Bowen drag Fletcher out of a shady-ass house on the outskirts of town. The guys he'd been with ... they were dangerous. How my youngest brother even got involved with them, I have no idea. But it had taken brute force and a ton of paper towels to Bowen's truck after Fletcher passed out on his floor and we'd had to scrub the puke from the floor mats of the cab.

"What time is it?" When I talk, it feels like my voice is treading over broken glass.

"Six a.m.," Bowen says as he pours himself a mug of steaming hot coffee.

"Can I get a cup of that? Or an IV, preferably." I rub the sleep dirt out of my eyes and shake my head as if that will solve the conundrum of my family.

Bowen walks across his open-concept first floor, past his kitchen island and into the living room I slept in. Where my house looks like it's just missing the wife, two point five kids, and white picket fence, Bowen's is all bachelor pad. Male furniture, simple design, little personal effects adorning the walls.

I take the mug with a nod of gratitude. The hot, magic power of the brown liquid sliding down my throat somehow brings me half back to life. To the point where I can finally come to terms with what this day will bring.

"Where is he?"

Bowen stares straight ahead. "In the shower. I told him to wash the vomit off."

My head drops into my hands as soon as I place my coffee on the end table. "How the fuck did we get here, Bow?"

He just keeps looking at the wall. "I don't know, man. He needs help. We've tried before … but this time, it's worse. These people, Keat, I know some of them from … before. They're dangerous."

I don't need to ask what he means. Upstairs, the pipes shut off, and whether or not we're ready to confront Fletcher, here he comes.

"Gentlemen." He has the balls to smirk at us as he comes downstairs dewy-eyed as a schoolgirl.

Bowen is up and across the room, pinning him to the wall in three seconds flat. "That's how you're going to approach this, dickwad? You're a piece of shit, you know that? Not only did you almost get us killed last night, but you also ruined my fucking truck! And you have the nerve to come down here smiling?"

I can tell that Fletcher is having trouble breathing, and he's scratching at Bowen's hands where they pin his neck. Rushing over, I smack at Bow's arms.

"Bowen, let him down!"

He releases Fletcher, and my youngest brother drops to the floor in a heap.

"You don't know what it's like! Neither of you do. I don't just get loaded, drink two handles of liquor and vomit or piss on myself, for the fun of it. I can't stop this ... *this* urge. It's part of me. Booze is like air to me, I need it to function. I can't just stop."

Fletcher buries his face in his hands. A moment later, Bowen looks at me with the most pained look I've ever seen on his face. Our youngest brother is sobbing.

I go to him, kneel down. "Fletch, I know you can't help it. You're an addict, you're sick. I'll never know what that feels like, but I do know that there are ways you can get help."

He throws his hands up, distraught. "I've tried before. All of that AA shit, rehab, *all* of it ... it doesn't work on me. I don't need Bowen to choke me out to know that I'm killing myself."

Bowen joins us on the floor, a move that surprises me. "Fletch, you might not remember what I did, but I've been close to where you are. I know it feels like nothing can stop this, that you're in too deep. But you're not. As long as you're breathing, there is a chance for you to turn it around. Come on, brother, do this for us. Do this for *Mom*."

I almost add that he should do this for Dad, but I think that would be laying it on too thick.

Fletch shrugs and mumbles, "I can try."

I'm not convinced, not in the least, and I know we'll have to stay on him for a long time to come. But right now, I have to get to my office and sort out a few things before I head to my mother's house to help her with projects.

After consulting with Bowen on next steps—calling a friend who suggested a rehab center near Lancaster and keeping an eye on Fletcher for the next twenty-four hours—I get my work done by noon and then head for my childhood home.

The minute I walk in the door, I smell *home*. That distinct scent my parent's house always has, that just settles in my bones. But this isn't home anymore. There aren't baseball cleats by the door or water guns hidden in between the books on the living room shelves.

"Why was there a message on the answering machine from Jerica Tenny?"

*Christ.* I knew she'd corner me at some point during this visit, but I didn't think I'd be in a shit storm this soon.

Mom was the only person I knew who had a landline answering machine that actually voiced the messages aloud.

And shit, I should have given Jerica my number. She's the town's premier realtor, and I've been in contact with her for two months now about possibly listing my parent's home. Except ... I'd never told Mom about it. My brothers and I agreed that she needed to move and that we all couldn't keep up the maintenance with a house most of us didn't live in, and none of us wanted to care of.

"Well ... I've been talking to her about possibly listing the house." Why does it feel like I just shot myself in the foot?

And why the hell do I always have to be the one having the hard conversations? Where is Forrest, who was unreachable last night? Why can't Bowen give a shit enough to do this? When will Fletcher grow the hell up and help out around here? I'm so damn sick of taking care of everyone ... and yet I'll keep on doing it. Because that's what I do.

"Keaton William Nash. *How dare you?*" Mom looks like I've sliced her in two, that's how much pain shines in her eyes.

"Mom, please don't fight me on this. Not today. I already have enough shit going on with Fletcher. Please, just let a realtor come take a look at the house and tell us what it might be worth, or if it needs any fixing."

She frowns. "What's wrong with Fletcher?"

I roll my eyes, reaching my breaking point. "We're really going to pretend we don't know that he's a major alcoholic and needs to go into rehab? Come on, Mom, like I said, not today."

I'm never this harsh with her, but maybe I need to stop treating her with kid gloves. Nothing ever gets done around here in the time it should because I'm always being cautious not to step on any toes.

"Keaton William, don't speak to me that way. I ... I know your brother has a problem. But ever since your father passed ..."

She dissolves into a puddle of tears, and guilt instantly swamps me. I gather her in a hug, her head hitting just below my shoulders.

"I'm sorry, Mom. I am. I know it's been hard for you." I pat her back the way she always did when we were sick as little kids.

Straightening, she wipes her eyes and walks around the living room. "I know I have to sell it soon, it's foolish to keep such a big house now that there is no family in it. But ... this is my home, Keaton. Your father built this place for me. How am I supposed to leave it?"

Right then, it dawns on me that I've finally become an equal to my parent. She's coming to me for advice.

I take her by the shoulders and decide to give her the truth. "You're going to leave it. Because I know this is going to hurt ... but that chapter of your life is over. You're only sixty, Mom, you have so many years and adventures left ahead of you. You are way too wonderful of a person to sit in this house and mourn the ghosts in it. It's time for all of us to move on ... it's what he would have wanted. Dad would be so disappointed if we kept his memory alive by sitting in this house, feeling sorry for ourselves. He'd want you to go out and *live*."

She nods, squeezing my arms in what I know she thinks is a gesture of thanks, but to me feels like she's holding on for dear life.

"Tell Jerica that I'd like to meet with her. But I'm not selling this house to just anyone, my boy. It's raised a good family for a long time. Someone is going to honor that memory."

# 19

It's Monday, which means one thing.

The shop is a goddamn *madhouse*.

Townspeople of Fawn Hill sure do love their mail and packages just as much as they love their books. If it isn't someone who wants to send three packages overnight through FedEx, it's the old woman who comes in for a stack of new release hardcovers each week and tries to haggle down the price. I wouldn't complain if I didn't like it, though. The residents are quirky; the work is fast-paced, and spending time with Grandma in the shop is a nice perk.

The line has been almost out the door all morning, and I've had three people get mouthy with me. Grandma just argues right back at them, like it's a sport she enjoys, but I'm not as comfortable yet. My adrenaline is at its peak for hours, because I know people are watching as I race around the store trying to check customers out as accurately and quickly as possible.

By the time I get a minute to catch my breath, there is one more person in line, and I turn to help them.

"Hi, there, how can I help you?"

It's not until I push my hair behind my ear that I see who it is.

Keaton stands there in his usual work polo and khaki shorts, and he's even added a stethoscope to the mix that shouldn't be sexy but it so is. His hair looks like he's been running his fingers through it all morning, and I didn't realize the weight of anxiety sitting on my chest until right now, when he made it disappear.

How strange was it that I'd never really thought twice about a guy before, and now I couldn't *stop* thinking about this one? Maybe there was some truth to that stupid little ... something ... at first sight.

"I was wondering if I could take you to Kip's for lunch?" His hands splay wide on the counter, and damn if I haven't been dreaming about what those might do to me once we're alone again.

And with the way those chocolate eyes are scanning me like a barcode, I'd say he's been dreaming about *things*, too.

Grandma walks out of the back, shooing me away. "Get out of here. A handsome man asks you to lunch, you go to lunch."

"Are you sure? If you need help restocking after the madness, I can stay to help."

Over the last couple of weeks, I'd seen just how bad my grandmother's eyesight had gotten. She could barely read now and had mistaken two people for someone else last week when they walked into the store. Grandma has lived in this town for over sixty years ... there was no way she forgot a face. Unless she couldn't see it. It worried me more than I could say, and I knew that a decision was going to have to be made about the future of the store. And since I was the one here, it terrified me that I was going to have to make it.

"I'm not blind yet, Presley. Get out of here." Grandma's tone is clipped.

I know she doesn't want sympathy, but I can't help it. "All

right. I'll see you in an hour or so."

As soon as we're out on the street, Keaton takes my hand in his. It's warm and strong, and the touch sends goose bumps running up my arms.

"It's good to see you."

Even though Kip's is only two blocks from my family's bookshop, and even though we're in the middle of the sidewalk where anyone could see, Keaton stops mid-stride to pull me into a hug. My breasts collide with his solid chest, and I'm enveloped by strong arms wrapping around my waist.

It isn't until right now that I realize I've been waiting to be back in his arms. That, all too quickly, Keaton is becoming the person I want to talk to when anything happens during my day.

My arms lace around his neck, and I inhale the clean, male scent of him. Pressing up on my toes, I place a quiet, gentle kiss on his cheek as I nuzzle my nose into his jaw and hear him sigh.

We're embracing in the middle of the street, and I'm sure someone is staring, when my stomach rumbles. He pulls back, smirking.

"Hungry?"

"Very." I laugh.

He takes ahold of my hand again as we walk to the diner, and once inside, he grabs menus from the booth and waves to the waitresses and cooks. I wave too because most of them know me now. We walk back through the narrow restaurant and he chooses a booth in the back.

"This was my dad's booth." Keaton says it simply, sliding into one side like we've talked about his father before.

I swallow and try to retain my composure because I know this subject is heavier than the weight he's giving it.

"It's the perfect spot, corner booth with the best angle on Main Street. I can see why he chose it."

A small smile plays on his lips. "Yeah, I guess Dad always did command the best."

"What was he like?" I ask as we sit across from each other.

Keaton reaches for my hand and I give it to him, our arms crossing the table. Before he can answer, Jaime, one of the waitresses, comes over to ask what we'd like for lunch. I order a BLT and an iced tea while Keaton opts for a buffalo chicken wrap and plain old water.

Once she leaves, he looks out the window, concentrating on Main Street.

"My dad was the ultimate family and community man. Loved my mom, raised four boys with a strong but gentle hand. Attended church every Sunday. Did pro bono work for a lot of the farms around here. Started his own business and built it from the ground up. He was healthy, never complained, and had this sense about him ... it was like he could see right through every answer you gave him. I swear I used to think he was psychic or something."

"Did you always want to follow in his footsteps?" I suck some iced tea through the straw immediately after Jaime sets our drinks down.

"Yes, although he may have groomed me for it as his oldest, I have always loved animals. My dad wanted out, he'd done his time and the minute I graduated from my medical program, he had one foot out the door. His stipulations were six months of us working the practice together, and then he was gone. I mean, I'd been working in the office, and with animals, since I was twelve. It wasn't as if I was unequipped to take it over ... but I guess I didn't realize how quickly I'd be running my own business, let alone be a solo doctor in a practice. And then, six months later, he died. Left so suddenly that I couldn't ask him all of the questions I had about our profession. All of the questions I had about life."

He might be a grown man, one who acts unflappable and is

the picture of a jovial guy, but I can see the sad little boy grieving in there.

I squeeze his hand. "I'm so sorry, Keaton. I have no idea how hard that must have been for you, how hard it still is."

Finally, he pulls his eyes away from the window and back to me. "That's why I work as hard as I do. It's why I try to stay on top of my brothers and help my mom out whenever she needs it. That's what he would have wanted from me, the oldest son, you know?"

This upstanding, responsible man sent my world into a tizzy. How the heck was someone so noble ... interested in me? I was in awe of his strength.

The conversation fizzled into surface level talk when our food was set down, plus I didn't want to push him. Keaton had decided to open the door that I suspected he kept locked up tight even if it was only a crack. I was grateful, and if I played it right, maybe he'd feel comfortable enough to tell me exactly what went on in that gorgeous head of his.

"Don't you need to get back to the office?" I look at the clock hanging on the wall with a cut-out to see right into the kitchen.

It's been nearly two hours, and it's the middle of a workday. This is so unlike the Keaton I've known so far.

He shrugs. "I told Dierdra to shuffle some patients around. It's no big deal ... I wanted to spend a long lunch with you. Are you trying to get rid of me?"

This makes me chuckle. "Maybe ... no, I'm not. I'm kind of flattered that the upstanding Dr. Nash changed his schedule around for me."

"Only for you. And, just to be fair, I've done a mental checklist of what I need to get done by the end of the day about fifteen times since we've been sitting here." Keaton's smile lights up his face.

"I'd expect nothing less."

# 20

Presley and I spend most of the week together.

We see each other for lunch, either spending it at Kip's or with brown bags on a park bench. I teach her about the butcher shop's deli meat, and she brings me bread that Hattie buys from the Amish market half an hour away. She tells me about her life in New York, and I listen intently, trying to gain insight into what makes this woman tick.

What I've learned so far? Presley is independent but seeks affirmation. She's also one of the kindest and most open-minded people I've ever met. She hates mustard but likes to put pickles on any kind of sandwich and even told me that peanut butter and the sour vegetable isn't a bad combination. Even though she doesn't hear from them a lot, and I have a feeling there is more of a backstory to it, she loves her family. And her laugh is the best sound I've ever heard.

On Friday night, I had her over for dinner at my place for the first time. Having a woman back in my house was ... strange. But it only took a minute for that feeling to pass, and then we split a bottle of red and cooked tacos together, and it had been the best night I'd had in ... well, maybe ever.

The night had ended with us on the couch, her shirt on the floor, and one beautiful breast fitting perfectly in each hand. I'd jacked off twice after she insisted on leaving, and I was still semi-hard as I pulled on my workout shorts this morning.

Presley left because we were both trying to pace ourselves even if we didn't say it out loud. As much as I wanted to drag her upstairs and strip her naked, I held back. We were having a good time, what was the rush?

However ... just because we were pacing ourselves didn't mean I couldn't surprise her at her class this morning.

I lock my front door and pull a ball cap down over my head; the brim shielding my eyes from the Saturday morning rays.

"Tell me again why I have to come to this?"

Forrest was sitting in one of the rockers on my front porch, in almost identical workout gear.

"Because I haven't seen you in a while and you're my brother. Plus, you're getting a little pudgy around the middle."

Forrest stands, lifting his shirt to show me his abs. "You don't know what the fuck you're talking about, old man."

I smile, shaking my head. "To be so young again. Ah well, you're coming with me and that's the end of it."

"Whatever. I'm really just going to this thing because there are going to be a lot of women in yoga pants. Bending over. And it's a nice day."

Rolling my eyes, my annoyance at my brother sparks. Forrest is always the hardest one to keep in line. "Hey, where were you the other night, anyway? I haven't seen you in a week. Fletcher needed you."

I might be scolding him, but I'm the older brother and that's my right. Forrest has always been the fringe sibling, the one who operates best without us all.

"Do we have to be up in each other's fucking business all the time? We're grown men," he grumbles.

See? He's fiercely independent, which is strange for someone in such a tight-knit family, much less a twin. But he could live on his own in a completely new place and guarantee, we'd never hear from him. I found out he went to London last year when I couldn't get ahold of him for two weeks and we finally asked the travel agent in town who'd booked the trip for him.

And he's so damn smart, so much smarter than any of us. It gives him an advantage, and grates at me as the oldest brother and head of the family now.

We walk over to Bloomsbury Park together, since I live so close, and my brother's eyes light up as soon as we crest the hill to the field where Presley's yoga class is located.

And there she is, standing in a group of women all wearing some sort of yoga legging or short and tank top combo. Presley has opted for the short, the magenta spandex highlighting every curve of her well-sculpted ass. They're paired with a tight white athletic tank top, and how I'm going to get through this class without an erection is a mystery.

"No you didn't." When she spots me, she starts laughing and points to the rolled up yoga mat I carry under my arm.

"Amazon for the win, baby." I shrug, making my way to her as the women around us watch.

"Hey, Forrest." Lily waves at my brother, and then at me.

Despite what happened between her and Bowen, I know that Lily is an amazing girl. She was great for my brother and really did nothing wrong. But what she doesn't know is the shit that went on behind the scenes ... and how Bowen really *did* protect her. His rejection of her, his ignoring her, it's for her own good.

"Lily." Forrest nods and then turns to Presley. "And we met briefly, but I figured I should get to know the woman my brother is dating."

A few whispers crop up when my brother says this, and I

wink at Presley. The people in this town have already been talking about it, this much I know from patients who come in and flat out ask me if I'm seeing the McDaniel girl. But to have my own brother come out and confirm it ... the women in this yoga class can't wait for it to be over so they can go blab to anyone who will listen.

I don't mind though, let them. Presley and I know, without having to have a middle school conversation about it, that we're only dating each other. And I'm pleasantly surprised that for the first time in two years, I want the town of Fawn Hill to know what's going on in my love life.

"Nice to meet you." Presley shakes Forrest's hand. "Hope you're ready for a workout."

The smile she wears is downright cocky, and I feel my dick twitch in my shorts. *Down, boy, we have to get through this without embarrassing ourselves.*

My brother looks skeptical. "I'm just surprised this took off so quick."

"Don't be an ass, Forrest Nash. Presley is really great at teaching, and this town needs to get with the twenty nineteen workout craze. Lord knows some of the residents here could work off that pie from Kip's," Penelope, one of the young PTA moms and an all-around town queen bee, chides him.

Again, my brother lifts his shirt, much to the delight of some of the women standing around. "I don't think I have that problem."

"Put your abs away, wonder boy." Penelope rolls her eyes.

I pull Presley aside for a minute, and as soon as we're out of earshot, I give her a quick kiss on the cheek.

"It's okay that I'm here? I wanted to surprise you, see you in your element, but I can go if you want me to."

She lays a hand on my arm. "Keaton, I want you to stay. If only so I can kick your ass."

"Only if you massage it later. I have a feeling I'll be sore." I advance toward her playfully.

"Enough, Casanova. I have a class to teach." She pushes my chest with one hand and walks off.

It is a sight to watch her go.

Only, ten minutes into the class, every muscle in my body is straining.

"I'm using muscles I didn't even know were fucking there," I whisper to Forrest, rubbing my calf as the whole group bends over in some salutation.

And even though my tendons are on fire, I can see why the yoga class is so popular. The reason? Presley. She's enigmatic while also being a calm, soothing presence over the class. She knows her shit and explains in a quiet voice as she walks around, helping people with their poses.

The whole thing is actually relaxing, but works your body, which I guess is the goal.

"My shit doesn't bend that way." Forrest eyeballs the ass of the woman in front of us.

"Just ... try your best," I say, exasperated.

"If my ball sack splits open, you're paying for the plastic surgery."

The woman next to us giggles, and another gives us a death glare.

There isn't supposed to be much talking during yoga, and yet my brother apparently never got that memo.

"If the gentlemen in the back can't keep it down, I'll have to ask them to leave. This class is for quiet meditation, thought and health."

Presley smirks at me from her mat up at the front, and I nod my head in apology.

I sure do hope I get that massage later. And that I can reciprocate.

"So, you're replacing me?"

Ryan's bitter tone comes through the speaker of my cell as I draw a perfectly winged eyeliner stroke across my lid.

"Shut up, I'm not doing anything of the sort. Plus, you could never be replaced. Who would retrieve all of my passwords when I lock myself out of websites?" I chuckle.

"You're technologically hopeless, but I still love you. So what's the deal with these chicks? And when are you coming back to the city?"

I bite my thumbnail, anxiety racketing through me, and thank God Ryan can't see it. Because I wasn't sure I was ever coming back to the city. I'd only spent two months in Fawn Hill, and one of those had been without knowing anyone but Grandma. Now that I had a life here—a job, my yoga class, blossoming friendships and a man I was dating—I honestly couldn't imagine leaving. In the city I'd had nothing but misery, one-night stands and the craziness of twenty-four hour noise in my brain. I would have never expected it, but Fawn Hill was quickly becoming a place I could see myself staying for a very long time to come.

"The *chicks* are Lily and Penelope, and I met them when I started teaching my yoga class. Lily is in charge over at the library, and Penelope has three kids even though she's our age. They're really nice and want to take me out for a girl's night. But you know you're still my best friend. We've been through too much shit together for me to ever cut you lose ... you might spill my dirty little secrets."

I choose to ignore the second half of her question. Not that I've told this to anyone yet, but I've pretty much decided to stay where I am for the foreseeable future.

"Pinky promise I'll take them to the grave. I have to go. This guy I met on Tinder is taking me to an escape room."

"You're going to an escape room with a guy you just met? Don't families get destroyed in those things? Isn't there a lot of yelling and working together?"

Ryan snorts. "Exactly. It'll be the ultimate test if we would be good together. And if we can't escape, then he definitely isn't coming back to my room."

Her absurd logic has me giggling long after we've hung up.

I swipe some red lipstick across my lips, pucker in the mirror, and run a hand down my navy blue sundress. I'm excited for this girl's night. When Penelope suggested she get a babysitter and drink Lily and I under the table at the Goat & Barrister, the only bar in Fawn Hill, I was all for it. My nights and days had been spent with Keaton and Grandma and having a little girl gossip would be fun.

My phone blinked nine o'clock as I got behind the wheel of Grandma's car. I still didn't have one, and she was fast asleep so she wouldn't miss it. I sent one last text to Keaton before I drove over to meet the girls.

Me: *Hope you're having a fun night on the couch.*

I snapped a selfie, making sure to highlight the V-neck of my dress, and sent it.

Keaton: *You look incredible. Have fun, be safe. If you need a ride home, call me.*

While I was happy to have some time with new friends, part of me wished I was sitting on that couch with him. Keaton's house was so cozy and having a place where we could be alone was a novel concept for me. Even though I was nearing thirty, I'd never had a place of my own, detached from other apartments or devoid of roommates. Spending time with Keaton made me feel more grown-up.

Parking is located behind the bar, and when I walk into the Goat & Barrister, Lily and Penelope are already seated atop barstools. The place is part British pub, part Pennsylvania dive bar, and I appreciate the charm.

"Hi ladies." I sidle up next to them, putting my purse on the bar and climbing onto the stool next to Lily, who now sits in the middle.

"Hey, girl, thanks for coming out." She smiles.

Penelope holds up her drink. "Catch up. Mama has a babysitter for another hour and a half and then this princess turns into a pumpkin."

Her sarcasm makes me laugh. "I have zero idea how you manage it. I can barely take care of myself, let alone three kids."

"TV and chicken nuggets, the secret to parenting." She downs the glass of wine in her hand.

The bartender, a surly old man in a flannel shirt, even though it's July, comes by to take my drink order. I ask for my usual, a nice, dry glass of white, with an ice cube. He obliges, and sets it down in front of me in exchange for my credit card to start a tab.

If I'd asked for an ice cube in my wine back in New York, some hipster bartender would have rolled his eyes at me. But here, I just get my drink, no side of judgment.

"I think that might be the secret to single life, too, because I do that often." Lily giggles, taking a sip of her light beer.

"Amen, sister. Although give me a pint of ice cream any day."

"You're not single, get the hell out of here. You've got the oldest Nash wrapped around your finger," Penelope scoffs.

I smile, unable to hide my happiness. "I don't know about that, but ..."

"He did yoga for you." Lily raises an eyebrow.

"Speaking of the Nash men ..." Penelope's eyes swing across the bar to a table near the dart board.

Three men sit there, all with varying looks of Nash genes. Of course I saw them all at the Summer Kickoff Carnival, but not up close and not for very long.

One gets up from the table, his swagger echoing across the room.

This is the brother Keaton left to go help the other night, I'd put money on it. He's younger than Keaton, and me by about three or four years from the look of him. Charm oozes from every pore, and he's more of a pretty boy than his brother; more muscular, almost as tall, but his hair is darker and his eyes are a sea glass blue that makes me think of the trip when my parents brought us to the ocean in Florida.

I can see how this young hotshot is the life of the party. The megawatt smile, the way he leans into women all over this bar. But you can see the gait in his walk, like he's on his sixth beer when everyone else is on their first. I can see the bags under his eyes and how he keeps taking shot after shot, as if the alcohol won't puncture his veins until he's at the bottom of the bottle.

And all at once, worry swamps me. I may not have directly dealt with an addict, but I've had friends and colleagues who have. I know how hard it can be to love someone with the disease, and how difficult it is to support but scold them all at the same time.

Keaton is the head of his family, and the anger that washed over his face at the water tower the other day makes sense. This has been going on for a long time, if I'm correct in observing his brother.

"Presley! Hey, you're the one banging my brother." His brother spots me and starts to make his way over.

Instantly, my face heats at his assessment of me.

Lily rolls her eyes and Penelope holds up a hand to stop him from getting too close. "Fletcher, go sleep it off. You're drunk, just like you are every time I see you. If Keaton heard you shooting your mouth off like that, he'd shut it for you."

Fletcher, now I remember his name, has the decency to look guilty. "Sorry, Presley. I just get excited that Keat is finally dating someone. He's just the best, my brother, you know?"

He's like one of those drunk college girls praising everyone when they're hammered. I should know, I was one.

But I'll take it. "He is. Nice to see you again."

"But tonight, he's lame. Didn't want to come out with us … said he didn't want to intrude on your girl's night. You should call him up, tell him to get his ass down here."

As soon as he suggests it, the other two Nash brothers make their way over. I recognize Bowen, Lily's ex, the brooding one with ghosts always in his eyes. He takes one look at her and falters. Then there is Forrest, Fletcher's twin, who came to my yoga class and talked the whole way through it.

"Good to see you both again." I smile at them, feeling weird because I'm technically dating their brother but we've never spent time together.

Especially without said brother.

"Hey, good to see you, Presley." Forrest nods. "I'm sore as hell, by the way. I have a feeling yoga isn't my thing."

"Yeah, considering you talked the entire time." Penelope smirks.

Laughter bubbles in my throat. "Yeah, maybe it isn't exactly your thing, but I appreciate you attending with Keaton."

"Got him wrapped around your finger already, huh?" Fletcher grins.

"He is pretty smitten." Forrest chuckles.

"Way to make me blush, guys." I take a sip of my wine to disguise my awkwardness.

It's the last in my glass, I'm surprised to find, and I flag down the bartender for another.

"They're just letting you know that he's happy, and we're happy for him." Bowen's gruff voice holds no happiness, but I know he means it.

His eyes keep straying to Lily, who looks like she is trying to melt into her barstool. You can cut the tension between these two with a spoon, and I feel so bad for them that my heart actually aches.

"I'm going to uh ... I'll be right back." Lily bolts, her strappy, summer sandals clacking as she hightails it across the bar and away from the man who broke her heart.

A stream of anxious breath whooshes out of Bowen, and Forrest claps him on the back.

"So, your brother didn't want to crash my party?" The thought is a little funny.

Keaton is starting to understand me. If he'd shown up here with his brothers, the place I'd told him I was going for a girls night, I probably would have been pissed. But while I'm glad he's given me my space, I also kind of want him here. We haven't done the group hang thing, and with all of the Nash men here, who look so much alike, it makes me want to see his face.

So I whip out my phone to text him. After I shoot off the message, I see Bowen's phone ding.

"Damn, you really did summon his ass. He told me he'll be here in two. Asshole was probably waiting around to be invited."

Forrest and Fletcher laugh at Bowen's mocking of their brother, but I'm too busy trying to calm my fluttering heart.

It seems to happen every time I know I am about to see Keaton. My whole system goes haywire, and I can't keep my hands still. Even now, the anticipatory tremor that moves through me feels like an electric current that could only be channeled when he walked into this bar.

"So much for girl's night," Penelope mumbles.

Forrest sidles up to her. "Fuck girl's night. I can do you one better."

She almost spits her drink out. "Forrest Nash, you're a boy. I'm a grown woman with children and a mortgage. In your dreams. Plus, I saw you get pantsed in elementary school, or did you forget that?"

The group cracks up at her scathing rejection, and Forrest pretends to have been shot.

But all the air leaves the room, at least for me, when he walks in. Maybe it's the two glasses of wine I've had, or that we've been talking about him for the last fifteen minutes and it's made me antsy. But as soon as Keaton's eyes meet mine, I don't want to be here at all.

I want to be alone with him, undressed, learning all of the things he can do with those capable hands.

"Hey," he breathes, coming directly toward me.

His hands go around my waist as he presses his lips to mine, in front of everyone. The worry about PDA goes right out the window though, when my mouth registers his warm one bearing down on it. I'm lost, my brain fuzzing over with desire.

There is a turning point in every relationship, that moment you know you're going to have sex. It's not a flowery way of putting it, but you know the minute you want to fuck someone, that the animal attraction is so strong you can't be satisfied with foreplay and anticipation anymore.

Tonight is that moment.

## 22

KEATON

"**N**o fucking in the bar!"

Fletcher's annoying fucking voice interrupts my tongue from entering Presley's mouth, and when I pull back, I'm mesmerized by the desire-filled green pools swimming before me.

"Nice to see you, big bro." He claps a hand over my shoulder, *hard*.

Turning, I watch as he sways in front of me. He's wasted, and I'm both pissed at my other brothers and surprised Gerry hasn't thrown him out of here yet.

"You should get him home." My disdain is made clear to Forrest.

I don't want to deal with Fletch tonight. For one, I wasn't even supposed to come out. I'd been watching the game, waiting for texts from Presley, trying to leave her alone. And for two, now that I was here, the only thing I wanted to do was take my girl home and give her exactly what her eyes were signaling to me.

She was going to let me have all of her tonight, I could feel it in the air.

"Don't come in here and piss on our party. We were all

having a great time. That is, until Lily scurried off like a scared mouse. Big bad wolf Bowen sent her running." He cackles, and everyone else in the group looks uncomfortable.

Forrest slugs an arm around his twin's shoulder and steers him away from the bar. "Let's go get some air."

Fletcher protests as they walk outside but follows anyway.

"Sorry you had to see that." I turn back to Presley. "I hope he wasn't too obnoxious."

She shrugs, smiling. "All is forgotten. I'm just glad you came down here. Thank you for giving me my space, though."

"Oh, get on with it, already. We got her for two drinks, now you can take her to bone town." Penelope rolls her eyes. "At least one of us should be getting laid around here."

Bowen chuckles. "Get out of here, man. Plus, you don't want Gerry seeing you."

Presley looks up quizzically at me, but it's too late.

"Thought I told you not to come back in here." The gruff harrumph of a voice is directed at me.

"Actually, you told my brother that." I purposely hug Presley tighter to me, which doesn't go unnoticed by the old man behind the bar.

"And yet, I've seen that drunk in here tonight." His glare could fry eggs. "And who is this?"

Suddenly, I don't want to tell him who Presley is. Even if he thinks his daughter did me a favor by leaving, I don't want the shit that's going to come with Gerry knowing my business.

"We were just leaving." I grab Presley's hand and nearly pull her off the barstool.

"Hey!" She swats at me until we get outside and I release her.

Being forceful with a woman is very unlike me, but the fight-or-flight instinct went off like an alarm bell in my head and I panicked.

"What the hell is wrong with you?" She rubs her hand, which I probably bruised.

"I'm sorry, here let me see ..." I take it in mine, gently, and rub the skin there.

"Jeez, Keaton, you looked like you'd seen a ghost back there." Presley palms my cheek.

I hang my head, disappointed in myself. I'd ruined our night in three seconds flat. She'd been having a good time, I was prepared to have a fun night with my brothers and the girls, and I'd turned it all to shit.

"Because I had. That was my ex-girlfriend's father ... Gerry, he owns the bar. It's why I don't go there if I can help it."

She nods, not letting go of my cheek. "We all have baggage, Keaton."

I don't want to talk about my ex or her asshole father, so I make it about something else.

"And then there is Fletcher. Jesus, he's a mess, Presley. And I can't seem to fix it."

"You know, you don't have to be everyone's hero. Your brother is an adult ... his mistakes, his problems, they don't have to be yours."

How I wish it were that simple. If I could just ignore the gorilla of responsibility my father left on my back when he passed ...

"I can't." My eyes bore into hers, pleading with her to understand.

Presley nods slightly. "Which is why you're such a good man. But, Keaton, sometimes I think you're too worried about taking care of everyone else that you don't take care of yourself."

I don't want to talk about this. She just doesn't see that if I don't do these things for my family, for my community, no one else will. I've always carried this burden.

So I cease the talk. "You could take care of me."

Stepping into her space, I don't give her the chance to respond. I'm done being the hero tonight. I want to take instead of give. I want to feel only pleasure, and I want so desperately to watch those green eyes as she feels hers.

Darkness surrounds us as the languid, hot summer air kisses our skin. My tongue invades her mouth, nothing cautious or searching like our other encounters have been. I'm tired of being the gentleman, of giving her patience and soft romance. I want her in the primal way a man wants a woman, splayed across my bed as I stroke in and out of her body.

"I want to take you home. I want you naked, under me. Please, get in the car." My voice is gruff, and Presley's knees wobble as she hightails it to the passenger seat.

Good thing we live in a town with very few traffic lights, and very few people on the roads after nine p.m., because I would have run them all and could have possibly gotten us killed. With one hand on the steering wheel, I've been caressing Presley's cleavage the entire ride while she suctioned her lips to my neck and her hands snuck into my lap.

By the time we make it back to my house, I am so hard that my dick can probably cut Captain America's shield in half.

Presley rounds the car and almost tackles me before I catch her around the waist. We stand in my driveway in the dark; her straddling my tented jeans, while our mouths take out every last frustration weighing us both down.

I kiss her with the fervor of a man starved and thirsty, like I've gotten my first taste of water in years and I won't stop until I've drunk so much, I'm sick. Presley gives me just as much passion back, rubbing herself against my groin as her hands tangle in my hair.

"I want you. Now." I breathe into her mouth.

This woman makes me crazy. I carry her up the steps to my porch and back us into the front door, pressing her into it as we kiss softly, slowing down while I fish my keys out of my pocket.

"A little hard, huh?" She half-moans, half-teases.

She's talking about how difficult it is to get my keys out of my jean pocket, but just to make her swallow her joke, I press my pelvis into hers. The movement elicits a pained groan, and I know I've served her that spoonful of snark right back.

Finally, after what feels like hours, I jimmy the damn door open, slamming it shut with my foot as I mount the stairs up to the top level of my house. Once I'm on the main living floor, I head straight for my bedroom, only halting when Presley's hands begin to pull at my T-shirt, begging it off.

"You want this off, huh?" I smirk, holding her around the waist with one arm while using the other to grab the material at the back of my neck and pull it over my head.

Presley deflates into me like a lust-drunk balloon. "Dr. Nash, did you just pull a porn move?"

"Maybe. Did it turn you on?" I can already see the answer in the dim lamplight of my bedroom as I set her down on wobbling legs.

Those green eyes spark as they take in my bare chest. "More than you know."

We're only inches apart, but in the time I'd set her down and turned the light on ... my body missed hers like we'd been separated by a continent. And while I wanted to do this fast, good God did my cock want to release into her right this second, I also wanted to take my time. This would be the first of many nights with Presley, of that I was sure. I was about to have this woman in the most intimate way possible, and now that she was giving me all of her, I was not going to let her go anywhere.

Christ, I was half in love with this woman and she'd only just come into my life. I was the epitome of that saying, "we plan and the universe laughs."

Going to her, I take her waist in my hands, massaging the cloth there until she begins to lift her arms, signaling that I should take off her gauzy white tank top. I oblige, slipping the whisper of material up, up, up her body and over her head. I have to clench my ass cheeks together inside my jeans when my eyes rake over the woman in front of me.

I've seen Presley naked before ... hell, she's been in my house naked. But this is more charged ... the air is thick with sex and impending orgasms. I can taste it on my tongue, and I want to take the charged tip of it and lick right up her seam.

She reaches behind her back and unclasps the tan, lacy bra holding her perky breasts. The undergarment falls away, and my fingers trace her skin, racing to see which can cup each perfect handful first. The color of her here is paler than the rest of her, outlined from the sun and free of those adorable sun freckles she gets. Her breasts are like pure cream, sweet vanilla ice cream topped with the ripest cherries.

I bend, using my teeth to pluck her right nipple, relishing her groan of pleasure and pain right before I suck it whole into my mouth.

"Keaton ..." She sighs, her body sagging against me.

We're chest to chest, our skin creating more friction than an electric current, as I move us to the bed. Before I climb on top, I help her out of her jean shorts, smoothing my hands down those long legs until Presley is writhing on the bed, reaching for me. She's an offering, lying atop my comforter and sheets in nothing but a white lace thong. From here, I can see the wet, bare flesh of her core, and I bite my lip as my cock jerks once more in need of attention.

Only when I strip myself, Presley watching with such heat in her eyes that I nearly come when I tug myself free of the zipper, do I go to her.

Muscle over flesh, pure male molding to the delicate flower, we mesh. After a few kisses that threaten to burn up the atmosphere, I lick and taste down her body. The elegant crook where her neck meets her shoulder, the dip of her navel, the lace hem of her thong.

"I've been dreaming about tasting you for what feels like a lifetime." I breathe into the fabric, inhaling her scent.

She squirms, looking down at me with half-mast lids. My cock brushes the cool material of the comforter, and I almost jerk with the need to seat it deep inside her.

My fingers trace the flesh above the lace, listening as each brush has a moan bursting from Presley's throat. And then in one fluid motion, I pull them down, away, and bury my tongue in her dripping core.

She rears up, a guttural sound filling my bedroom as the sheets bunch in her hands. "Ahhh!"

Her taste is musky, it makes me dizzy as I fuck her with my tongue. My hand moves to my cock, just holding the wanton member on primal urge. Eating a woman always gets me to the peak of arousal ... something about having their thighs hold my head like a vice as they shamelessly ride my face is the biggest fucking turn on imaginable.

My tip is leaking by the time I insert a finger into Presley, my teeth scraping her clit.

Unintelligible words and sounds mix with the heartbeat thrumming at the center of her body, and I keep my rhythm, winding her up to pop.

No more than a second later, her body arches with the grace of a jungle cat, chasing her orgasm through time and space as it wrecks her. As it makes her it's prey. She is ethereal, all of that red hair splaying across my pillows like a heart bleeding its feelings.

I can't wait any longer. As she's coming down, I grab a condom out of my bedside drawer and roll it on, hissing at the contact. My body covers hers, the need to make us one so thick that I'm choking on it.

And the moment I slide into her, my tongue loosens, the words that have been stowed away deep in my heart making it to the surface.

"How did I go through life not knowing that you were meant for me?" I breathe, looking down into her eyes with wonder.

My cock twitches inside of her wet, tight, hot folds, and when I slowly pull out and push back in, Presley whimpers.

"Completely."

She whispers the word, and at first, it doesn't make sense. But as I stroke her, gently at first, it clicks in my hazy brain. We fill each other, *completely*. The others before, they only half fulfilled us. We were only living half existences.

Removing the hand that's been roaming my abs, I pin it back, holding it to the bed. The move has Presley arching her back, thrusting her core up into me. I'm so deep that I'm hitting the back of her wall, and I know we are on the verge of explosion.

My hips shake as I pound into her, letting all logical thought fly out the window. I'm chasing the high, the release, and Presley goes off with a shout and scratch of her nails down my spine. The pain vibrates down my flesh and sparks a reaction in my aching balls.

And then I'm obliterated. I lose myself, collapsing on top of this angelic creature as I give all five senses to my climax.

In the end, all I see is red. She's hypnotized me, and now, I am hers.

"Why does this town celebrate the Fourth of July ... well, after the Fourth of July?" Presley shakes her head at the stage, food and game booths, and local business tents set up on the high school athletic fields.

Fawn Hill has its traditions, and most of them hadn't changed in decades.

"Ever since I was a kid, I've always celebrated the July Fourth holiday on July eighth, or somewhere around there depending on what day of the week it falls. The high school fields are the only place big enough or safe enough to hold all the towns-people and keep the fireworks at a safe distance. Since they have summer school during the weekdays, they don't want to hold them on a school night. And the organizers especially don't want to have to test beforehand or clean up after. A couple years running, when I was in elementary school, some teenagers would steal the displays or grab the exploded shells out of the field. So now, they wait for the weekend and have crews work overnight to pick up all the debris."

"Who knew Fawn Hill had such a rowdy teen population?" She wags her eyebrows.

"When you live in the middle of nowhere, you create your own fun."

We walk hand in hand past the different vendors, a local band playing a country song as people line dance in the dirt in front of the stage.

"Aren't you supposed to win me a teddy bear or something? Isn't that what boyfriends do?" Presley lays her head on my shoulder.

"Oh, I'm your boyfriend?" The thought lights me up inside like someone's just pressed all of the elevator buttons and I'm rising to the top.

"Wouldn't you call yourself that? I mean, you are sticking your—"

I put a hand over her mouth, trying to contain my laughter. "There are five-year-old's right next to you!"

Her green eyes are cunning. "Finger in my pie. That's all I was going to say."

My lips meet hers as we walk. "I'm *sure*. But ... if you want to call me your boyfriend, I'd be honored."

"What are we, teenagers?" Presley giggles.

"Sometimes I feel like it when I'm with you." I shrug, leaning down again to whisper in ear. "However, teenagers do not know how to fuck each other the way we did last night."

I feel the shudder that moves down her spine and has her rubbing her thighs together. "Keaton Nash, you are shameless. And yet, everyone here assumes you're some kind of saint. Imagine what they'd think if I told them what you did with your mouth last night."

Any of the girls I've dated in the past would have paled the minute I talked about fucking, but this woman just eats it, spits it out and serves it right back to me.

"That's for your body and your body alone to know."

"Oh, Keaton! I'm so happy to see you've gotten a new girl-friend. Shame you wasted so many years single and sulking."

I turn to see the three old ladies who always run the sweet corn stand during the fireworks festival and try not to bristle.

Presley's mouth, however, is hanging open. She's not used to Fawn Hill and its forwardness, or the nosy people who live here and assume your business is their business.

"I was just holding out for the right girl, Mrs. Jenkins. Ladies, this is Presley."

The woman on the left, who dyed her gray hair an unnatural shade of black, waved me off. "Oh, boy, we know who she is. Hattie's granddaughter, and she teaches that new-fangled exercise class in the park. An out of towner … not sure about her yet."

She says this as if Presley isn't standing right there, holding my hand.

But my girl, she just puts a hand to my chest and smiles at the gossiping old women.

"It's nice to meet you. I know I've been hogging the good doctor here, but you can rest assured I like Fawn Hill more than I like him."

Two of the women flash small smiles while the one who made a comment about her scowls.

"You're a pretty, young thing, aren't you? No wonder Keaton likes you. Look at those legs, Bertie!"

Mrs. Jenkins elbows Bertie, the one who hadn't spoken yet.

Bertie unabashedly checks Presley out. "A mile long. God, to be young again. I used to be able to wrap my legs around a man's waist—"

"Bertie!" Mrs. Jenkins swats her friend's arm.

Presley and I look at each other, bewildered and hysterical.

"Those hips look pretty sturdy to me." The scowling lady inspects me.

"Oh my God ..." Presley cracks up, turning her head into my shoulder and biting her lip to keep from howling.

"Good to see you, ladies." I'm about to lead Presley by the hand when Mrs. Jenkins interrupts us.

"Um, sonny, you're not going to buy your girlfriend the best sweet corn in all of Pennsylvania?"

Presley looks up at me sternly. "Yes, Keaton, you're not going to win me a teddy bear *or* buy me sweet corn? Maybe I need to find another boyfriend."

"I'll take him off your hands." Bertie's grin is all dentures, directed right at Presley.

I relent, buying us two ears of sweet corn doused in butter and parmesan, and hand one to my girl.

We bid farewell to the kinky old ladies and walk off munching on our cobs.

"This is delicious," Presley says, butter glistening on her lips.

That does something to my insides as I lead us over to the football field where most of the town has already laid down blankets to claim their spots. Just like I did earlier, knowing all too well how territorial people were on this night. I spotted the green-and-blue plaid blanket I'd set down and stepped over lawn chairs and George Foreman's to get there, careful to avoid the odd running child.

Presley sat on one side and I joined her, finishing my corn and wrapping the remains in the foil cone it came in.

"You've been every year, haven't you?" She smiles at me.

"Even when I was too cool and in high school."

"I keep forgetting this was where you went to high school." She finishes her corn and mimics my actions from a minute ago.

"Right over there is where I sat in the dugout during games."

She rolls her eyes. "Is someone trying to impress me with his glory days?"

The sun has sunk past the tree line, swathing the field in

darkness, but the sky is still light enough that the fireworks display won't start for another hour or two. Either way, I move in closer to her, closing the small space between us on the comforter. I move so that she's sitting in between my legs; her back to my front, and wrap my arms around her waist.

Like this, I can bury my nose in her hair and nuzzle past it to the soft spot on her neck that makes her shiver when I inhale there. As if on cue, a small ripple moves down Presley's limbs, and she swats gently at the hand secured on her stomach.

"You keep doing that and this fireworks show is going to be anything but G-rated."

"Is that a promise?" My voice comes out husky.

"Cool it, hotshot. Tell me more about your golden boy days." She turns her face and those green eyes flash up at me in amusement.

I laugh. "I was pretty much the same. Too concerned about grades, colored inside the lines and always did the responsible thing. I was pretty okay at baseball ... Bowen was the superstar, actually."

"Hmm, somehow, none of this surprises me. Remind me to make you play hooky from work one day, you have a lot of catching up to do. Why didn't Bowen go pro?"

I know it's Bowen's story to tell, but I can't just brush her off. "He was in a bad car accident. Broke his clavicle, couple of ribs, right arm, his left hand and leg. After that, his body didn't function the same in the sport."

She goes quiet in my arms and faces forward again. "The accident with Lily, right?"

Imperceptibly, I nod into her cheek, where I place my own. "It's not my story to tell."

Presley settles back against me again. "I'm not asking you to. You're a good brother, Keaton."

"So, what do we do until the fireworks start?" I change the subject.

"Are you asking for a little football field nookie?" Presley tilts her head back to look up at me.

"I have always had that fantasy. Maybe a little over the pants hand job action?" I whisper in her ear.

"Seriously? Keaton Nash, the good boy vet, is asking for an OTPHJ?"

Her acronym has me cracking up. "Yeah, I guess there are children around. And we wouldn't want to scare the nice sweet corn stand ladies."

"Or the Amish pretzel people." She snickers, and I know she's thinking about me coming in my pants while the strait-laced Pennsylvania Dutch stood selling their wares just feet away.

"You make me crazy." I growl.

Because she does. Presley brings out the real me, the man I never knew was there.

Life before her was muted, and with her in my arms, I saw nothing but fireworks.

## 24

I have a *boyfriend*.

The concept is so foreign that sometimes, I find myself just giggling at nothing.

Not to mention, I have a boyfriend who was a sex god. Like ... no joke, honest to ... well, God ... sex god. Who the hell would have thought, Dr. Keaton Nash, the small-town vet, would be an animal in bed.

A shiver runs over my flesh, causing goose bumps to rise, just thinking about the nights we'd spent in his bed. Endless hours of touching, different positions, those dark eyes pinning my soul to the bed just like he was pinning my body with his ... it all melded together to make me a mushy pool of lust.

But our time spent together was more than just fucking, more than just the physical release. The way that Keaton's gaze bore into me ... it was like he was reading my most inner thoughts. Like he saw how deeply I felt about him, but that I couldn't say the words out loud. Not yet.

Part of me was terrified. I didn't know how to navigate this. I'd fallen so completely ... gosh, there was that word again, for him in such a short amount of time that it almost felt like it was too easy. There had to be strife, hardships ... right? Love wasn't love without having to fight for something. At least that's what society tells us.

Maybe, though, there are love stories where a girl just meets the guy she was always supposed to fall in love with, and they do the damn thing.

I don't know. I'm too sexed out to think straight.

Unfortunately, said sex god did have to work, damn his responsibility complex, and that meant I was on my own on a Saturday. Penelope was busy with her kids, and Lily had some official event with her father, who was a state senator. I hadn't known that until recently, and from the looks of his website, which I'd visited, he was a total square. No wonder Lily gave off the whole daddy's girl, sheltered vibe.

So I found myself driving out of Fawn Hill, through the Pennsylvania country roads, watching the summer sun sparkle as the breezy air flew through the open car windows. Living in the city, I forgot how much I liked to get lost in the car. In high school, I'd drive out of my hometown and just take random turns, seeing where I'd end up.

Those were usually days when my sister earned some academic achievement, or my brother scored a goal on the soccer field to win the game in the final seconds. My shame wasn't born out of jealousy, it was created from a deep need to be seen as well. I was the average middle child, and my parents only had so much time. It was easier to sink into the background than exhaust myself trying to put in effort for pride.

But it came at a cost. Slowly, that unintentional invisibility chipped away at my confidence. So ... I began to distance myself. First with my drives. I'd take long, winding journeys, sitting on the hood of my car until the sun went down just thinking about what my life might look like in ten years. I didn't have a lot of people I trusted back then, or none I really wanted to confide in about how I was feeling.

I took it a step further when I moved out to the city. I was a nameless face in a sea of millions, and I kind of liked it that way. My family didn't keep tabs on me, and I didn't have to check in just to be disappointed when I didn't measure up in their eyes.

All of that, though, it leads to a sharp loneliness. And so my journey brought me back to the start. Maybe not to my nuclear family, but to where my family essentially started. When I used to sit on the hood of my car, imagining what my life might be like, I never in a million years thought I'd be living in a place like Fawn Hill. I never imagined I'd be falling in love with a small-town boy or cherishing the quiet peace that a place like this brings.

As I navigate Grandma's car down this country road, and over one-lane bridges, I make snap decisions about where I'll venture off. That's the fun about having no plans and going with your gut. I'm still that girl, the spontaneous nomad who enjoys living without strings. Falling in love and staying in one place doesn't have to change that.

I can still have adventures.

It's just that, now, I have someone who might want to adventure with me.

A road shaded in a canopy of trees catches my interest up ahead, and I turn onto it. The car steadily climbs, up and up the inclining road, the forest pulling me away from civilization.

And then the tree line breaks and the road becomes gravel. I have no idea why it's led up here, or what purpose this road serves. But I do know, that when I get out of the car, it is the most beautiful place I've ever been in my life.

I stand at the top of a massive, rolling hill, looking down into a valley. The landscape opened up, strokes of greens, blues, and yellows painting the canvas. A river rambles through the middle of it, cutting the farm fields in a babbling flow of water. I could spot cattle grazing, and the sun beat down as if its attention was directed solely on me in this moment.

There was a chance that I would only come to find this paradise once, and I'd made a promise a long time ago never to catalog or map my aimless drives. Because the point was to find a special place in that moment, and if life brought you back to it, then it was a sign of something bigger.

After sitting on top of that hill alone for what felt like hours, I picked myself up and dusted my hands on my jeans. I hadn't thought about *anything* for that time, and it felt good. Sometimes, you just needed an afternoon where no heavy questions were asked, no feelings were examined, and you could just sit with yourself like an old companion.

When I got back in the car, I drove toward home. Today, an aimless journey was necessary. And normally, my brain would rebel against the act of settling back into a routine.

But not today. This time, when I knew the journey was coming to an end, I was happy to be going home.

# 25

The smell of sizzling hamburgers and Frank Sinatra's voice fill the air, accompanying the fireflies flashing their butts around the humidity of Keaton's backyard.

Sitting in one of the Adirondack chairs on his patio, I watch as my boyfriend mans the grill.

"You hold that spatula like you know what to do with it." My eyebrow cocks up suggestively.

Keaton turns, waving the utensil through the air. "Once I've cleaned and dried it, maybe we could put it to good use."

"In your dreams. Is my burger ready yet, I'm starving!" My stomach grumbles.

Keaton chuckles. "You have less patience than a hungry puppy. I just put them on the grill. Enjoy the night air, drink your wine. Listen to Frank."

"I'm not sure I get the allure of Frank ..."

He whips around. "I'm going to pretend you didn't say that. The man is a legend, the ultimate man's man. He's an icon, a—"

"Jeez, you've got a real hard-on for a crooner who has been six feet under for over twenty years," I tease.

Keaton turns back to the grill, mumbling about a certain woman who has no musical taste.

"Let me take you to my kind of club in New York City. The rap lyrics busting out of the speakers will melt your face off they're so good."

He shakes his head. "How can we be so different?"

"Opposites attract, baby." I get up from my chair, walking to him and wrapping my arms around him.

I press up on my tiptoes to rest my chin on his shoulder, looking at how he layers the cheese on top. It begins to melt instantly, and my stomach grumbles again.

Keaton's pocket vibrates, and I'm all too aware of what that means by now.

If it's not Fletcher pulling him away, it's a veterinary crisis. And on another occasion, his mother called in hysterics after watching the home movie of her wedding.

I hadn't been kidding the first night we slept together when I'd said he took care of everyone. The guy was like Superman, piling damsels and distressed persons alike onto his back and trying to carry them to safety. Meanwhile, no one looked back to see if he was crumbling under the rubble of the disaster.

Keaton wanted to help everyone, and I saw how much that wore him out. How tense his shoulders were after a day in the office. The lines of anger and helplessness in his face every time Fletcher got wasted after swearing he'd never touch a drop of alcohol again. And the monstrous grief of his father's death, that he kept hidden from his mother to spare her more sadness for herself.

"What is it this time?" I tried to keep the hint of annoyance out of my voice.

"An ewe has gone into distress while trying to birth baby lambs at one of the farms on the outskirts of town. They need me to come out and help."

He stares down at his phone, thumbing through pictures that have obviously been sent to show him the situation.

And all at once, our relaxed evening on the patio is gone. He's in Dr. Nash mode. He's in hero mode. He's already turning off the grill, taking the hamburger patties off distractedly and putting them on a plate. I watch them bleed juices onto the white ceramic as I try to keep calm.

This is how a life with him will be. We may be in a small town, but he's always going to volunteer for anyone who needs saving. It's an admirable quality, but what is the line he won't cross. Will he leave in the middle of the night when I'm in our bed? Put a patient or his brothers over future children? It sounds insane thinking these things, but ... I've never had a boyfriend before. And it's pretty serious between Keaton and I if I'm in a relationship with him, something I've never done with another man. These are things I need to consider.

And I need to consider if I can be okay with them.

"I'm so sorry, Pres." He turns to me, his dark eyes begging for me to understand.

Swallowing my concerns, I step into him and pull him against me for a minute.

"I am, too. But we can take our burgers to go."

Keaton stills. "You want to come with me?"

I nod. "If you'll let me. I want to see what you do. And I'm here to spend the night with you, no matter where that takes us."

Awe, and a bit of storminess, shine down on me as he pins with me his gaze. "This could get ugly. We could lose the babies, or the ewe herself."

The thought sends an arrow of sadness straight through my heart. "I'm a big girl. Let me come to work with you. Seeing your passion, it will help me understand you better. And I want to understand everything about you."

Keaton looks like I just told him the secret to life. "All right. But when we get there, you stand back. Only move if I ask you to. Got it?"

I crack a small smile. "Yes, sir." He frowns, and I roll my eyes. "Of course. I'll keep out of the way unless you need me to hold a leg."

We're there in twenty minutes flat, thanks to Keaton's speeding. We munch on burgers on the way, eating them one-handed as he details what a twin animal birth can be like. How many he's seen, what he might need to do for this lamb after looking at the pictures the farm staff sent. Listening to him talk is addicting; even if I know nothing about veterinary medicine, the way Keaton talks about his craft is admirable.

Once we arrive, darkness swamping the fields and barns of this small dairy farm, Keaton goes straight for his trunk.

"Here." He hands me a rubbery looking suit that I realize after a few seconds are goulashes. "They are probably going to be big on you, but if you want to be in the pen, you're going to want those on."

I don't talk, trying to digest everything that's about to happen. I don't mind a little blood and guts, but I've never witnessed a human birth, let alone a large animal. Part of me was downright scared, and the other was tingling with excitement.

Keaton pulls out a large case, almost like a toolbox, and then shuts the trunk, walking toward the only dwelling with lights on.

"Remember what I said." He looks down at me with softness.

I nod and then see his face change. This is the doctor in him, the man who needs to put emotions aside to save the animal in need. He can't hold my hand right now, and this is his way of telling me that if I can't handle this, I have to take care of myself.

The dwelling with light is really just a small barn, gated off by large pens where I assume animals are kept. Right now, though, there is only one animal in here, and she's crying out as if someone was stabbing her. The guttural, anguished sounds of the sheep penetrate my heart and make me suck in a lungful of breath. Anyone can hear and see how much agony she's in ... and I just want it to stop for her sake.

Keaton makes quick work of getting brought up to speed by the farm owners and then jumps right in. He examines the sheep, getting down next to her. From my vantage point, I can see something sticking out of her vaginal opening, and it looks ...

Well, I'm no medical professional but it doesn't look good.

"I'm going to have to get in there and pull the lamb out myself. It's going to hurt her, you'll need to hold her." Keaton's voice is the epitome of calm.

Two of the men move toward the animal while Keaton pulls out a few tools and a needle full of something that he injects her with. I hope to God it's the best epidural a sheep can get.

Something in me moves without a thought passing through my head as if my limbs are on autopilot. I go to her, this wounded female animal, and take a hold of her chin, directing her eyes up and into mine.

"Shh, baby. It's going to be okay." I stroke her fur rhythmically.

"All right, hold her steady." Keaton's fierce eyes flash to me.

We all hunker down, and I try to keep my focus on her pained eyes. The minute Keaton begins to deliver the baby, I feel it radiate throughout her body. Her limbs go stiff and start to shake, and the sounds coming out of her throat are a hundred times worse than anything I've ever heard.

"Hold her!" Keaton snaps, and while I can't see what he's doing from my vantage point, the frustration on his brow is making me nervous.

What feels like a lifetime, but is probably only another

minute, later, I hear the sigh from the mama sheep and a mewling cry from what must be the baby Keaton helped her deliver.

"All right, mama, one more." Keaton strokes her belly.

There is a lapse between the babies, and I feel the animal breathe some relief. She's gathering strength, regaining some of her wits now that the pain of the botched delivery is subsiding.

"She's contracting. Here we go!"

The compassionate, thorough vet, the one I met all those months ago, is deep in the middle of doing what he does best. To watch him in the environment he excels the most in ... it's an honor. Watching Keaton work is an art form.

With one last push, grunts emitting from her throat, the second lamb slides out.

"Good job," I whisper in her ear, a tear of joy sliding down my cheek.

Being in that moment, with this animal and with the man who helped her through it ... it was breathtaking. There is a buzz in the air that pierces straight through my body. It's life itself, creating sparks of electricity all around us. I've never felt more invincible, or more human. The juxtaposition is so intense that I might start to weep.

I stand, moving to the side of the pen as the farm owners and hands tend to the mother and babies.

"That was incredible." I breathe, clutching my chest to make sure my heart is still beating.

He comes toward me, pinning my back to the wooden wall of the stall. His lips cover mine, his gloved hands staying at his sides. I'm not even worried about the slime and blood getting on me, which is odd, but ...

I can only focus on the single point of contact. His mouth on mine. Possessing it so wildly that I might pass out from the assault.

The kiss is brutal and passionate, a lifeline connecting the two of us. Keaton stokes my body like it's a flame and he's an arsonist, just from the skilled use of his tongue and teeth.

We just watched life being born, a soul come into the world. It was beautiful and painful, all of the emotions mixing into one.

Only when one of the newborn lambs whimpers does he pull away, his forehead pressing into mine.

"You just keep surprising me." The words are whispered reverence.

My eyes stay glued to his, words failing me.

Keaton swivels his head around to check on the baby lambs. "Let me tend to them. Go wash up and I'll meet you back at the truck in ten."

I take the opportunity to go wash up, because as much as that was incredible, no one likes the stench of blood and afterbirth on them. I hose down, even spraying some of my hair because the night is hot and humid, and my blood feels like lava. Something about watching a life come into this world has my adrenaline jacked to eleven.

Ten minutes later, Keaton joins me where I sit on the hood of his truck.

"Thanks for coming out here." We aren't touching, and both of our gazes look off into the dark fields beyond.

"That was truly amazing, Keaton. How do ... how are you so sure of yourself?"

I think that's the thing I both envy and love about him. He always seems so confident in what he's doing. I can't even pick out tea without changing my mind six times, and yet he could be thrown into a burning building and get everyone out alive without questioning one move.

A small laugh emits roughly from his throat. "Isn't that the show I put on? Truthfully, I'm better at acting confident than actually being it. If you fool yourself long enough into thinking you know exactly what you're doing ... at some point, those around you start believing it. Even if you know, deep down it's a lie. That's my dirty little secret if you want to know the honest truth of it. I pretend to be the strong leader, my actions show a level-headed, responsible man who knows the correct path. But inside, I'm just as goddamn scared as everybody else. I lie awake at night wondering if my life means anything; if I've made the right choices. I'm not sure of myself, Presley. It's a house of cards. One stiff breeze and I come crumbling down."

His confession shakes me to the core, and I feel the raw honesty ripple through my gut all the way out to my fingertips. They tingle as I try to wrap my mind around something. Because Keaton admitting that he's just as scared as everyone else, that his confidence is a lie, doesn't make me want to run from him.

That feeling I'm trying to grasp? It's bottomless, hopeless love. The kind I have no shot at falling out of. This man, the one I originally thought couldn't hold a candle to me or my fast life-style, has opened my eyes to a world of feelings I'd had no idea existed within me.

But instead of confessing that, I decide to give him just a small piece of me back.

"Sometimes I wish I could go back and tell my seventeen-year-old self that she was enough. That she *is* enough. I grew up thinking that everything I did and everything I was just never measured up. I wish I could tell her that things get so much better. That she should laugh more and stop worrying so much about what other people think. I wish I could tell her that she doesn't have to have a conventional dream or even a conventional life. She doesn't need to move to a city and get a high-paying job. Most of all, I wish I could tell her that the strength she needs is already inside her if she would just open her eyes and look."

He doesn't speak, and our mutual confessions hang in the air.

At the exact same moment, we reach across the hood, our fingers lacing, the crackle of electricity between our hands the only response we both need.

## 26

KEATON

I hadn't felt like getting out of bed this morning ... so I
hadn't.

Presley had felt too good, and I was getting used to
waking up to her in my house. The past two weeks, since the
night a sheep's labor interrupted our backyard dinner, we'd
been inseparable. Aside from work, and the occasional family or
animal emergency, I was with her.

The redheaded temptress who made me laugh just as much
as she drove me absolutely crazy with lust. In almost three short
months, Presley had completely taken over my life, inserting
herself in all of my thoughts and every decision I made.

Last week, I'd told two after-hours calls to wait until my
office was open in the morning. I ignored a request from Mom to
come over and cut the lawn, instead passing the task off to
Forrest. Who, by the way, was still texting me bitching about it a
week later.

And Fletcher ...

While worry still needled my brain every five minutes I
thought about my little brother, my heart tugged me in the
direction of the kind, spontaneous woman who kept surprising

me around every corner. I hadn't heard from him in a week, and I was trying to be okay with that. I was his brother, not his father.

Like Presley had said ... I didn't have to be everyone's hero.

And now that I thought about and had spent the past two weeks living my life the exact way I wanted to—tangled up with the girl who didn't know yet that I was in love with her—I saw just how much my strength and responsibility were taken advantage of.

I wasn't just a helping hand or the stoic leader ... I was their errand boy. The fact that Forrest was complaining about mowing his mother's lawn for the first time in five years that I hadn't felt like doing it? It was pathetic. So was the fact that neither he nor Bowen had given me an update about Fletcher ... which meant neither of them felt the duty to keep an eye out for him.

Same thing with my practice. Did Nelson really need to bring his cat in at one a.m. on a Thursday because she'd had a little spasm in her sleep and then went right back to snoozing? And couldn't the wellness visit of a litter of puppies wait until Monday when I'd already gone to Gloria's house on Saturday—a weekend day I might add—to check that they were all healthy and thriving?

I'd trapped myself in this role of servant instead of the one of volunteer. I'd offered to help so much that my friends and family just expected it of me now ... they were abusing my kindness and caring.

And now that I had a woman in my life who was quickly becoming *more* than all of that ... I didn't want to get out of bed to serve the community who had been using me for a while now.

My hands slide down Presley's naked ribcage, and she whimpers in delight as the silk of her skin caresses my fingertips.

"Your body ... it was made for me to touch." I breathe, bringing my lips to the curve of her breast.

"You are a total tease." She chuckles on a moan.

My mouth hovers over her skin, never touching, but the hot air of my breath gets her worked up to the point that she's arching up to follow my lips.

We've been in bed half the morning, what with both of us calling out of work. It was reckless and immature, but I'd never done it and Presley had been daring me to try it for weeks, so here we were.

I have to say, with my hard cock in my hand, poised between my girlfriend's thighs, it was the best damn decision I'd ever made.

"What, no oral this morning?" Presley pants as I draw the head of my cock up and down her slit.

I press in, the tiniest fraction of an inch, making us both growl for more.

"You don't need it, you're already so wet for me," I grit out, my teeth clamping together as pleasure shoots down my spine.

And without warning, I sheath myself fully into her heat. The move temporarily blinds me, my vision hot white, and when I'm finally able to regain composure, Presley has her tits in her hands, massaging her own nipples.

The sight almost makes me shoot my load right there.

"*Fuck.*" I pull out slightly and push right back in, the small movement sending dangerous vibrations to my balls.

"I love it when you curse. Something about that dirty word coming out of that good boy mouth ..." Presley breaks off when I slam into her, her legs shaking as they tighten around my waist.

I drill her into the bed, my lips latching onto her neck, my intention to leave a mark. This woman of mine, she drives me to insanity. The springs of the mattress creak and her moans fill my ears, spurring me to move even faster.

"Get on your knees."

I want her from behind so badly; I see red.

Presley rolls over like a cat in heat, a fox who's being chased but wants to get caught. She positions herself for me, her red locks spilling over her back, and when those green eyes flash at me in challenge, I drive in to the hilt.

Holding her hips in my hands, I fuck her. There is no other word for what we're doing. It's hot, sweaty fucking in the middle of the day ... and I'm so turned on by how not normal this is for my everyday life that every sense beside those connected to Presley is dulled.

Which is why I don't hear it at first. Somewhere on the floor, probably under a pile of clothes, my phone starts buzzing. I ignore it as I'm ... currently occupied.

"Do you ... need to ... get that?" Presley gasps, her fingers digging into the bedsheets.

I shake my head, using my teeth to scrape across her spine. She tenses up, letting out a sexy, guttural moan as my right hand reaches around to nudge her right leg out farther, spreading her wider for me.

"No," I grunt, stroking harder now.

My hips roll every time I'm seated deep, right down to my balls.

Responsibility and worry try to claw their way to the forefront of my brain. Someone is calling me, and my phone won't stop ringing. My family, Deirdre, a patient ... someone is probably in need. But right now ... I don't care.

I'm in bed with a woman who has changed my whole life perspective, and I wouldn't pick up that phone even if there was a gun to my head. That's how much I'm willing to sacrifice to be with her.

"I'm going to come," Presley moan-whispers, and it's the sweetest sentence I've ever heard.

Not the sweetest sound, because that comes a moment later when she's burying her face in the pillows.

"That's it, baby, yeahhh ..." I coax her, wanting to draw out her orgasm as long as possible.

And when I feel the last of it start to leave her, I let go, jutting up against her perky ass and feeling the come burst out of my tip as her cheeks slap back against my groin.

I lose my breath, flashes of pleasure rolling over me, drowning me. At some point, I collapse onto Presley, our slick bodies one on top of the other.

"So, you happy you cut class now?"

Her mocking voice is granted a rough laugh back.

"Playing hooky is starting to grow on me." I roll off of her but take her hand and keep it in mine.

She plants a kiss on our joined hands. "I've created a monster."

In more ways than she knows.

"**O**h, fudge!"

Grandma's words follow a crashing sound that comes from the supply room.

I rush around the counter and across the store, into the back.

"I'll be right back!" I yell to the two customers checking out books in the fiction section.

When I get back there, a dozen boxes have spilled onto the floor and Grandma is kneeling among them.

"Oh my God, are you hurt?" Bending, I check to see if there is any blood or broken bones.

"I'm fine, I'm fine." She swats me away. "Just the damn box that was stuck."

Taking her elbow, I help her up and keep my hold on her just in case she's shaky. "What were you trying to get?"

"The damn box of packing envelopes," she replies crankily.

My heart stills. "Grandma, the packing envelopes are on the bottom shelf over there by the duct tape."

She's silent for a moment, and I know she either couldn't read the boxes she'd just knocked down, or she'd forgotten that's where we always kept those envelopes.

"I know that, don't tell me something I already know!" Her voice is ornery and aggressive.

But she didn't know that ... or at least she couldn't see it. And my heart breaks for her at that moment. It was probably terrifying not recognizing the shop you'd worked in for years. It was probably even more aggravating that your brain or body was failing you, and there was nothing you could do about it.

"Okay, why don't you go up front and check those customers out? I'll clean this up." I don't hug her, not wanting to make her feel more of whatever she feels right now.

I hold my breath until she leaves the stockroom and then release an emotional exhale that threatens tears at the tail end of it. She's getting worse by the day, and I don't think there is much time left until we have to make a decision about the store. About her life away from it.

After cleaning up the mess of boxes, I collected myself to face Grandma with a soothing smile. I found her in the empty store, skimming over the books in the historical fiction section.

"Did you know that your grandfather's favorite writer was Steinbeck, but I can't stand his books?"

She held a brand new copy of *The Pearl* in her weathered hands, staring down at the cover.

"Honestly, I was never much of a reader myself. But working here, hearing your stories about the pages Grandpa snuck while he was on the clock, it makes me want to be."

"You're a real good kid for coming here and helping your old grandmother out." She looks up at me, her eyes giving away the lump of emotion that must be sitting in her throat.

"Of course." I take her hand in mine, mentally preparing to be slapped or something. "Grandma, I think it's time you made some decisions about retiring. About what's going to happen to the store."

But instead of shrugging me off or talking back, she just nods her head.

"I know I do. So let's make them right now."

"Me?" I say in surprise.

"None of the rest of our family has bothered to bring their asses home to deal with it, so you get half of the say. For starters, I want to retire. Goddammit, I'm old. My bones ache and my back hurts from standing all day. I've already lost my partner, but I think I could still sit in a rocking chair sipping lemonade."

My heart thuds against my chest. "What is going to happen to the store then?"

"Do you want it?" Her question was point-blank.

This was it. Stay or go. She was asking, and I'd avoided answering it myself for two months.

"I ... I'm not sure." I was sure, but I wasn't.

This was all too fast. Was my life goal to go into owning a post office slash bookshop? Sure, I didn't mind working here, but forever? I'd barely come to grips with the fact that I wanted to stay in Fawn Hill, let alone run my family's shop all on my own.

"Well, maybe someone else can take over this shop." Grandma looks at me from over her glasses.

I stop stacking certain size envelopes on the shelf behind the counter. "What do you mean? This store has been in our family for decades."

"And now this old bird can't hack it anymore and maybe my family needs a new start." She clucks her tongue at me.

"What are you talking about, Grandma? You want to sell the store?" I'm thoroughly confused.

She sets the book back on the shelf. "You don't want to run this shop. We both know it. This isn't about staying in Fawn Hill, because even though you haven't said the words out loud, we both know you're staying here. But this shop isn't for you ... and that's okay. You've gotten that fresh start. Look how amazing your yoga classes are going. You've been running them for the past two months, and they're only growing. Hell, you have women from surrounding towns coming out to take a class from you. I think it's time you put your money where your downward dog is."

"Grandma!" My laugh is hysterical. "Where did you learn that phrase?"

She shrugs. "I listen to you sometimes when you're planning your classes."

"So what are you saying? I should start my own studio?"

The idea strikes a chord so deep in me that it vibrates through my entire body. It felt so ... *right*.

Grandma nods. "And you have your first investor right here. I'm going to put this place on the market tomorrow, how about that for a decision?"

"Grandma ... I can't ask you to do that ..." My skin crawls with anxiety.

She places her hand on my cheek and scoops it under my chin, tilting my head so that I'm looking directly into her wise, cloudy eyes.

"All your life, you've taken a back seat to other people's successes. Somewhere along the way, someone told you that you weren't good enough, and you believed it. In my time of need, you uprooted your whole life to come help me. And you've done it without complaint, you've not pushed me or taken advantage. Your nature is sweet and your spine is steel, and I know that I'm backing a truly good horse when I say I want to invest in you. I want to invest in making your dreams finally come true. No more taking the back seat, kid. You get to drive."

Tears spill onto my cheeks, but not at her offer to fund my dreams. She's right about it all but truly right about her first statement. I have always been told I was never enough. Even if it wasn't those exact words, the actions and neglect of those around me cemented that idea to my soul.

The fact that Grandma is so sure of me, proud of me, and willing to help me reach a goal I didn't even realize burned so passionately in me until this very moment?

It was the only thing I'd ever asked for coming true.

## 28

S eeing the for sale sign in front of the home my father built for my mother was somewhat surreal.

Having Presley here to see it, and to meet my mother as my official girlfriend for the first time, felt even more like I was living in a fantasy world.

"Mom?" I called as we walked in.

The house looked ... different. Where the overstuffed furniture and farmhouse charm had once existed, were now clean lines and the scent of a sterile, model home. Anyone who lived in Fawn Hill would walk in here and know that this was the Nash home, but it no longer held traces of little boy's school pictures lining every available surface or the advent calendar my father had carved for my mother that she kept hanging on the wall year-round.

"Wow, this place is ..." Presley breathes beside me, her head extending all the way back on her neck to look up at the cavernous ceilings and exposed wood beams. "You grew up here?"

I chuckle. "That I did."

"This is something out of a Georgian plantation." The smile on her face is goofy.

"Want to buy it? Only a cool five hundred thousand."

I really hoped Mom got the asking price for the house. It was the highest listing in the area, but this house was worth it, and we were hoping someone from out of the county would come in and scoop it up. There had to be a family from any of the nearby cities who had been considering a move to the country and would see my parent's home and fall in love.

My heart beats a nostalgic, sad rhythm when I think about someone else growing up here. When I think about other little boys hiding in all of its nooks, and about a mom rounding them all up to sit at the dinner table until they're excused. This house deserves that, and I know my own mom won't rest until a buyer of that caliber makes an offer.

"Oh, Keaton, good! I need you to—"

Mom is a ball of energy as she comes barreling down the hallway toward us with stacks of boxes in her hands. And the minute she sees the gorgeous redhead standing next to me, she shoves them into my arms.

"Presley! Oh gosh, my son didn't tell me you were coming over! I would have mixed us up a nice couple of glasses of my strawberry iced tea. Oh, I'm so glad you're here!" She hugs my girlfriend.

I bobble the boxes, peeking inside as one of the lids almost clocks me in the jaw. Photos, hundreds and hundreds of them, are stacked inside. She must have gotten these down from the attic ... which is a good thing because it means she's finally taking my advice to clean house. Literally.

"Oh, there was no need, really. I'm just glad I got to come over here before it sold to see the place where Keaton grew up."

"And I'm glad that my son finally got his head out of his butt and asked you out."

I raise an eyebrow at her. "Didn't you practically force me to ask her out by sending us up alone on a Ferris wheel?"

She waves her hands at me and motors past us into the kitchen. "I need to clean out a couple more things before the open house this weekend. Keaton, honey, could you get the boxes of China down from the upper cabinets? You know I never could reach those."

Presley sits at the counter as my mother uncovers the boxes I just set down on the island, and they're thumbing through pictures while I struggle not to drop priceless antique dishes. Being up here, cleaning out these cabinets, it reminds me of when my father would reach into the high places and take things down for my mother. How he'd tease her for living among a hoard of gangly giants, also known as her sons. And then she'd swat him and he'd wrap her up in a hug.

Looking back, my parents had their own language of love that I'd never noticed as a kid. The grief that always resided in my figure sighed with weariness. It lived in the ache in my chest, the set of my shoulders, the clenching of my jaw. After you lost a person so essential to who you were, their passing and the sadness of it took hold of your bones and muscles.

I know I was the one who finally convinced Mom to put her house on the market, and it was for practicality and her own sanity. But I hadn't understood what it would mean for me. Every time I walked over the floorboards, I thought about how it would be my last. The scratches on the walls where my brothers and I had knocked them playing tag, the creaky step we avoided when sneaking out ... the memories hit me full force. It's the end of an era, and I'm not manly enough to hide the sadness I feel.

Not that I'd ever admit that to my brothers. They'd probably punch me in the arm and tell me to grow a pair.

"Oh. My. God. Who is this cute little Dalmatian?" Presley

squeals with laughter as she holds up a picture to show Mom and me.

"That would be Keaton. It was his first Halloween, and oh, he was just as cute as a button." Mom takes the photo, covering her smile with a hand. "You loved animals even then."

I have to smile, too, because I was pretty freaking adorable. "I was the cutest baby of all your boys. Admit it, Ma, don't worry, none of the rest of them are around to hear."

"Oh, no you weren't!" Mom shakes her head like she's in a presidential debate. "Fletcher was the cutest baby."

Presley howls at my mom's diss. "Don't worry, Keaton, you're still the cutest baby in my eyes."

The glare I give her has her laughing even harder. I heft the last of the china boxes down and blow the dust off them, a little getting in my eyes and causing me to squint.

Mom takes the lid off one, and the gleaming white and silver of her set blinks back at us.

"Oh, they're gorgeous. How old are these?" Presley marvels, running a hand over one of the plates.

"They were my grandmother's. The set dates back to the early nineteen hundreds, and I've tried to keep them in the best condition possible so I could pass them on."

The way Mom is looking at Presley right now has alarm bells going off in my head.

"Now, I know I may have forced you two onto that Ferris wheel, and I'm about to jump to conclusions again."

"Mom—" I try to cut her off.

The thing Presley gets spooked about the most? Putting down roots. And my mom is about to play right into her worst fear.

"Keaton William, don't try to silence me. I know you two just started dating, and I know I'm an old woman who wants grand-babies and weddings and things you aren't ready for yet. So what I'm going to say is just an offering ... a starting point. I had Keaton get these boxes down because I am going to send them home with him. Him, not the both of you. They should go to my oldest daughter-in-law, which is why Keaton is inheriting them. But, that being said, I really hope that daughter-in-law can someday be you, Presley. I think you're perfect for my son, and I see the way he looks at you. So, this china is a promise, and I hope you'll see it as one, too."

My lungs burn, and I'm surprised to find that I've been holding my breath the entire time my mother speaks. When I look to Presley, I find tears shining in her eyes and a smile on her face. Which ... has to mean that she isn't completely freaked out by my mother basically proposing marriage to her as my proxy.

"Thank you, Eliza. Truly, this is very special."

I clear my throat. "Okay, now can you stop proposing to my girlfriend so we can empty this place out?"

That gets a laugh out of the two women, and I'm glad to have de-escalated the situation a bit.

Nothing like a mother's guilt to send your girlfriend heading for the hills.

## 29

"This might be even better than the yoga class we attend here." Penelope giggles as she tilts her chin up to salute the sun.

"Hey!" I spritz her with my spray bottle, which is the only thing keeping me hydrated out here. "I heard that yoga class was the shit."

"Teasing." She chuckles, sighing. "This is the best kind of day. Especially because my kids are at camp and I have a glorious eight hours to myself." Penelope wiggles on her towel next to me.

My skin burns from the sun exposure, but it was the good kind of burn. The kind that felt purely summer, with the heat beating down on you so much you could practically feel each new freckle sprouting up on your nose.

I'm not sure who volunteered the idea of tanning by the lake at Bloomsbury Park, but it was the best suggestion any of us had had all summer. Living in the city, I had to take two subways and a train to the nearest beach. Having a place to lie out right in my own backyard was something I'd have to take advantage of more often.

"I can't even imagine pushing a human out of my body." Lily laughs at her best friend, sitting up on her elbows to look at Penelope.

She's in a yellow bikini that highlights her fun-loving, cheery personality and also matches her long, curly brown hair that's threaded into a braid.

Penelope snorts. "You were there for the third, Lil, you saw it. It's not fun once, let alone three times. Also, your body will never be the same again. Every time I sneeze, I pee, and have you seen these stretch marks?"

The curvy blonde points to maybe two faint silvery scars on her tight stomach and sighs.

"You look like a Kardashian, only blond. So Khloe, but not as tall. Seriously, shut up," I chastise her.

"She's right. Now you only have to make a sex tape and you'll get famous." Lily laughs.

Penelope applies some more tanning oil to her supple chest. "Who says I haven't?"

Lily and I whip our heads to her. "You have?" We say in unison.

She just smirks, and I turn onto my stomach to tan my back. "I've always thought making one might be hot, but also I feel like I'd just be looking at the imperfections of my body jiggling the whole time I watched it back. And is it weird to watch your own porn?"

It's Lily's turn to frown at me. "Um, have you seen your body? You have like zero percent fat on you, plus people kill for your shade of hair. You're gorgeous ... and I don't think Keaton would object to watching your porn tape over and over and over again."

That sends a blush all the way from my toes to the tip of said red roots.

"How is Dr. Nash in the sack, anyhow?" Penelope asks.

I prop myself up on my elbows, totally game for a little sex talk with girlfriends. I've missed this, and I've never been shy talking about the dirty deed.

"The man may examine animals all day, but he knows damn well what to do with a woman. He's *very* generous. And I know he may seem like the mild-mannered small-town doctor, but in the bedroom, he is shameless. God, the things he does ..."

I fan my face just thinking about it. I would have never guessed that Keaton turned into a dominant heathen when the lights went down.

"So what she's saying is that he likes to lick her pussy, and then hold her down when he fucks her." Penelope takes a sip of water from her bright pink tumbler to hide her snide smile.

"Penelope!" Lily's voice is the peak of embarrassment.

"Oh, come on, little Miss Librarian. I've known you too long, you don't fool me. You've been with the most caveman of all the Nash boys, even if you were just in high school. You're a dirty little minx in the bedroom. I just miss sex, is all. Orgasms aren't quite the same when you give them to yourself."

"Tell me about it," Lily grumbles, relenting.

"What is it about having a man on top of you that is so satis-fying? Like not even the sex, penis in vagina, part of it. But the actual weight of him."

"It's because that weight on you is comforting. It's why people get those weighted blankets." Lily flops from her stomach to her back, shaking her feet in the grass where her towel ends.

"So what you're saying is that I should get a weighted blanket and a vibrator and I'll be good to go?" Penelope snickers.

"Or you could find an actual man. Come on, there are some pretty nice guys in Fawn Hill. Surprisingly. Come to think of it, is this like the hidden gem town of hot men?"

There were actually way too many sexy guys around here for

this place to be real. It was a blip in rural Pennsylvania, for God's sake.

"Must be something in the water." Lily laughs.

"An actual man, what a nice thought. Too bad I have three miniature humans ruining my life. I wouldn't even know where to fit a man in my house, let alone my bed. There is always a combination of kids or dogs in my bed ... I barely get any covers myself."

I eye her, because I've honestly never thought about being a mother. I guess in a someday sense I have, but I'd never been in a relationship, which I think makes you really consider the possibility of children. And now that I was ...

It would be lying to say that I didn't picture more little Nash boys running around.

"Is having kids really that bad?"

Penelope sighs. "It's not, I know I'm sarcastic and cold-hearted most times, but they are my biggest blessing. They're just a handful, and I was so young when I got married to Travis. And then losing him ... my two oldest remember him. They ask about him constantly. So on top of grieving myself, I have to deal with children who are grieving. Plus, they're just rambunctious in general. I don't wish I had a different life, but sometimes, I wish I had two hours to myself."

"Well, we're here if you ever need to get out. I'm happy to watch the kids, you already know that. Except for that one time they locked me in a closet and threatened to use said closet as a Nerf Gun target." Lily laughs, but reaches over me to squeeze Penelope's hand.

The death of her husband wasn't something she talked about often, if at all, but I knew he'd been in the military and died overseas. They'd been married since she was nineteen and had babies shortly thereafter in rapid succession. I couldn't fathom what it was like to lose the man you thought you'd grow old with.

"Enough with the pity party, back to the sex talk." Penelope takes my own spray bottle and squirts me with it.

I laugh. "What do you want to know?"

"How big is his thing?" Lily squeaks.

"Lily, I'm so proud of you." Penelope chuckles.

"And I may kiss and tell, but I don't draw pictures. Just know, he's both a show-er and a grow-er."

They both hysterically laugh, and I flop down with my face in my towel.

I was smiling too, but for a completely different reason. I'd had friends, homes, summer days in bikinis ... I'd had all of these things in the past.

But I'd never felt as comfortable in my setting or in my skin than I did right now.

That was something to smile about.

And just like that, summer is over.

The first day of September marks a change in the seasons, but also in my life. I've now lived in Fawn Hill for an entire quarter of a year. I've been through the hottest of days and wake today with the scent of autumn and orange leaves on the breeze.

Anxiety bubbles in my chest, leaving me with an unsettling feeling that at best feels like acid reflux and at worst feels like something I don't even want to put a name to.

Most of the day passes with much of the regular routine; breakfast with Keaton, my ten-minute walk to the bookshop, helping customers, eating lunch with Grandma, and meeting Keaton on the corner of Main Street so he can drive us home to start dinner.

It shouldn't be different than any other day ... but it is. I can't put a finger on this *turmoil* inside me, or maybe I don't want to. Because the creeping fingers of a toxic friend I thought were long gone are tightening around my neck, and I'm running out of air.

The suffocation started when Grandma came to me this

morning with a document that I didn't want to read. The sale listing for McDaniel's Book & Post. She'd done it, the thing she'd said she was going to do about a month ago. The shop she'd spent her whole life building, this family business that had existed in Fawn Hill for decades ... she was selling it to help me start my own business right here in the town she loved.

And I couldn't put my sneakers on fast enough. My hands were itching to tie those laces, to run. It was instinctual, a knee-jerk reaction that had me silently breaking down in the tiny bathroom of the store so that she couldn't hear me. I was trying to get a grip on myself, but I was slipping.

This happened every time. Every time shit got real, or life took on another layer, I got going. It's not like I wanted to be a quitter or a coward ... it was just something inside me that wouldn't be extinguished. Maybe in a past life, I was a gypsy. The thought made me hiccup as I'd sobbed in the McDaniel's bathroom and I knew I was only trying to gloss it all over with sarcasm.

T he feeling only intensifies over dinner when Keaton tells me his mother's house has sold in a matter of weeks. He's called it the end of a book and took hold of my hand and said we'll be able to start a new chapter. He says that his mom was going to take a small portion of the money she received from the house sale and split it between the boys. I could tell by the glimmer in his eye that he had an idea for what that money could be used toward ... and the butterflies born of nerves in my stomach grew tenfold. They'd already been placed there the day she offered me her china at the house, and now they were swarming.

By the end of the meal, all I want to do is get out of the

house. I am jumpy, anxious, my palms are sweating ... it is as if I've been arrested for a crime I didn't commit and am about to confess just to make it stop.

"Do you want to go out for a drink? Maybe put all of this change aside for the night, get totally blasted on a bottle of wine and do unspeakable things to each other?" I wrap my arms around Keaton's neck and attempt to give him the sexiest grin I can muster.

If we can just get back to the flirty banter we'd had going at the beginning of the summer, maybe I could relax. Today was too serious for me, too much heavy adulting going on and I couldn't cope.

Keaton's smile is far away, and when he looks down at me with those mocha eyes, I know he isn't thinking about alcohol and heavy petting.

He unwinds himself from me and crosses the room, setting his hand on the countertop, almost bracing himself.

"Remember Gerry, that old bartender that I had words with the first time you went to the Goat & Barrister?"

I nod. "The one you said is the father of your ex-girlfriend. Yeah, now that I'm not drunk and your brother isn't trying to fight someone, your interaction did seem odd."

That beautiful head of dirty blond hair bobs with his nod. "He snapped at me because he believed I was the one who trapped her here. Who made her not follow her dreams for so many years. Katie, the one who broke my heart the first time and did a damn good job of it."

My flesh bristles, the hairs standing on end. Something in me wants to stop him, wants to pause the tape right where it is so I don't have to hear about this. And I'm not exactly sure why.

Keaton continues without looking at me.

"We met when we were young. High school sweethearts, turned college couple, turned real-world partners. I thought I'd spend the rest of my life with her. We bought a house together, I was getting ready to propose. But I guess I never noticed how much she'd grown through the years. The long nights I was in medical school, the weekends spent away from her studying, and then when I went into my father's practice, I worked so much that we barely spent time together. She became a different person; where we once functioned as a unit, my schedule and life choices forced her to thrive on her own. Looking back now, the breakup was as much my fault as it was hers. We were too young when we met ... this town put a lot of weight on our shoulders. And Katie, she wanted more. She wanted more than to be the wife of the town vet, to be married to the only man she'd ever been with. Her interests changed, she started to dream. And one day, she left. Loaded up a truck and left town ... and I haven't seen her since. I was so angry, so heartbroken. I didn't understand it and I blamed her for a very long time. And I blamed her father, Gerry, for not helping me bring her back. I thought my life was going down the path that I'd always planned for it to go, and in one day, it was completely obliterated."

So many emotions roil in my gut. Heartache, for a younger Keaton. Jealousy, for some woman who could leave a man as good as he is. Apprehension, because I can tell where this is headed. And for all of my boasting about planting roots and feeling okay as a woman settled in once place, something in my chest begins to stir.

There it is, my old friend *flight*. From a young age, my flight instinct has been ultra-sensitive. It's sent me running anytime life gets murky, or complicated, or conflicted. It's the thing I couldn't put my finger on earlier, and now it's here full force.

I hate that this is part of who I am. I hate being the wayfarer, the one who can't buckle down in tough times.

"I thought she took my heart with her. But now, I know I was wrong. I was waiting for you to come into this town like the breath of fresh air, holding my heart right there in your hands. Katie didn't take my heart with her because it was never hers to have. Presley ... I was a fool for thinking that I ever loved another woman. Because that comes nowhere close to this. I've told you from the beginning that I'm a straight shooter, an honest man who plays no games. And it might be early, and lord knows it could get me in trouble with you, but I'm going to say it."

*Please don't*, I try to tell him with my eyes. This will ruin us.

"I love you, Presley. From the minute you brought that goddamn dog into my practice, I was head over heels. You balance me out in every way, and I don't know that I could have gotten through this summer without you. I am in love with you, and I know now that this kind of love was the one I was waiting for all along."

His confession feels like a bullet. Straight to the chest, mutilating my heart. I have to actively try to keep my feet planted to the spot, and words have escaped me.

Keaton just broke us, and he has absolutely no idea.

# 31

I knew when I decided to tell Presley I loved her that she may not say it back.

Hell, I knew she probably wouldn't. But stupid me, I'd given her the benefit of the doubt, just like I gave everyone.

And now she was acting weird. She'd said she wanted to have dinner with Hattie instead of coming back to my place as the week started, and now it was Wednesday and she hadn't slept over the first two nights of the week. She'd barely spoken to me when I brought lunch over to the bookshop and had shrugged off with some vague excuse about needing to see Lily when I asked if she wanted to see a movie tonight.

Inside, my gut roiled with regret and fear. I'd rushed things ... me and my stupid, small-town heart had told the adventurous, city-girl wanderer that we were in love with her. Which was basically the exact thing I knew would send her packing, and yet I'd done it anyway. Presley was distancing herself, and waiting for the other shoe to drop, waiting for her to tell me she couldn't do this anymore ... the anxiety was eating me alive.

"Keat, you've got to calm down." Bowen put a forceful hand

on my kneecap, stopping my leg that had been shaking a mile a minute.

"You're asking this man, who's only ever been with two women in his life, to calm down? Do you even know our brother, dude? He's going to work himself up into such a state, I wouldn't be surprised if he gives himself an ulcer." Forrest laughs at my misfortune and walks to my fridge, helping himself to whatever is inside.

"Hey, do not eat my leftover shrimp scampi!" I yell at him, chewing a fingernail. "And I have not only been with two women in my life, no matter how boring you think I am. I just ... the suspense is literally killing me. I wish she would just do it already. Break up with me. The avoidance or ghosting as you kids are calling it these days, is really messing with me."

Forrest walks back to my living room, a cold piece of pizza halfway to his mouth. "I could hack into her email or her texts. We could see what she's saying about you."

I glare at him. "No, thank you. And seriously, I mean no. Don't do it behind my back because you're bored."

He shrugs, already bored about talking about me.

"I get it, man, trust me I know what it's like to feel left in limbo. But you've got to just relax. And if you can't ... I guess you can track her down and make some grand gesture but something tells me that Presley isn't that girl."

How come in situations that don't apply to him, Bowen can be so articulate and supportive? Ask him one question about himself and he'll shut down.

"How's Fletch doing?" I change the subject.

I pick up the remote to have something to do with my hands and flip to *Planet Earth*. On the television, monkeys romp around in what looks like a tropical forest.

"He's actually doing well. Showed up for work this entire week, I checked his punch card online," Forrest tells us.

"I'm not going to ask how you did that." I stare at him.

But hearing that Fletcher showed up for work at the grocery store he took shifts at was encouraging. Maybe he was finally going to get his act together this time.

Forrest, however, was going to land himself in jail. My brother was too smart for his own good, and there were rumblings that he was attracting attention from the wrong kind of people. The cops were one thing, but Forrest stuck his nose everywhere it shouldn't be just for the sheer fact that he could. If he wasn't careful, he was going to get caught in a place he really shouldn't be one of these days.

"Hasn't been at the Goat, either. I checked with Gerry." Bowen leans back on the couch, checking his phone.

Who the hell is he waiting for? I don't think I've ever seen my brother remember his cell phone from the drawer he kept it in, in his bedside table, much less check it.

While I'd been buried up to my eyeballs in my infatuation with Presley, my brothers and our world had continued turning. I'd missed things, and annoyance begins to simmer in my chest. I was supposed to be the leader of this family ... I'd always known what everyone was up to and how everyone was doing.

I'd actively chosen, in the last couple of months, to take a back seat from my responsibilities. Something I'd never done before. And now that I'd confessed my feelings to Presley and she was shying away, maybe I'd temporarily walked away from my duties for nothing.

"Well ... that's good." There is nothing else I can say because, clearly, they have our brother handled. Without me.

"Listen, brother, can you see your life being any different if Presley up and leaves town? Like, you got by without her. Sure, you'll be butthurt for a while, but then you can get over it. And on top of someone else."

Forrest's question hits me right between the eyes. My life

*would* be different if she left. Honestly, the idea of her leaving makes me want to punch something ... and I am not a guy who's ever resorted to physical violence. Hell, I'm even a wimp when it comes to using Bowen's punching bag he keeps in his basement.

"You haven't been in love, man. You just don't get it." I smile at him in that sad, know-it-all way.

Because someday, the love he felt for some girl was going to slap him upside the head and shake all of those superior ideas out of that big brain of his.

"If that isn't the fucking truth." Bowen's eyes go stormy.

And it isn't until right now that I realize there are two breaking hearts in the room.

# 32

Two huge duffels lay open on my bed, their bodies are full of clothes as I meander through the disaster that is my bedroom.

I'm a coward. I admit it. The past week, I'd felt like I was living in someone else's life. My body didn't feel my own, I couldn't process things. My anxiety was maxed out at the highest level, and nothing—not work, or yoga, or walking through Fawn Hill—made me feel any better.

And so, I knew it was time to leave. I could go back to the city, get some waitressing job, crash on Ryan's couch. I'd be safe in that bubble, the fast, desperate lifestyle where no one could get too close and nothing was really tying you down. Everything was replaceable there; if you got fired, there were thousands of bars or restaurants who would pick you back up. Dates and men were a dime a dozen, nothing special could fill the void for a short period. There was no one who relied on you, no adult decisions that had to be made.

I needed that. Because I couldn't hack this. Sure, right now I was doing great. I had a steady job and the promise of a future in Fawn Hill. I had a man who loved me. But eventually, I'd screw those things up. Everyone around me would realize just how big of a fuck up I was, and it would all go south. So instead of sticking around for that, I was packing.

I was so wrapped up in my own thoughts and attempting not to burst into tears at any second that I didn't hear Grandma when she propped herself against my doorframe.

"Jesus, you scared the shit out of me!" I jumped as I turned around, spotting her from where I stood at my closet.

"What the hell do you think you're doing?" Her eyes were angry, narrowed buttons.

My heart was threatening to beat out of my chest, both from the fright and from her scrutiny.

"I ... it's a long story ..."

"Well, you best start talking, because I don't want to see what I think I'm seeing." She entered the room, threw one of my duffels sharply on the floor, and took its place on the bed.

When I didn't speak for a full two minutes, she threw her hands up.

"You're just doing the same thing you always do, Presley. I may not have been around for much of your life, but it doesn't mean I don't know what kind of person you are. You create busy work. You quit things before they're finished because it's easier. When life threatens settling or permanence, you shake like a leaf and run. Commit to something, dammit. You have a good thing going here, so pull up your big girl panties and do the work. You don't have to be a doctor or a lawyer ... but jeez, be *something*. If I had a dying wish, that's it."

Her words hit me right between the eyes and travel down to form an ache in my breastbone. They're harsh, they bite like a rabid dog ... but they're true.

"You're not dying. Don't go using that card to get me to do something." I roll my eyes at her.

"You really are so much like me it's scary." Grandma chuckles. "But I mean it, Presley. You're a bright, talented woman. I have a feeling my son and his wife didn't tell you that much while you were growing up. So, I'm telling you now. You can do whatever you set your mind to. That sounds like something you say to a little girl, but since you never heard, I'll repeat it. You can do whatever you set your mind to. Yoga studio, working in the bookshop, or whatever else floats your boat. Just give it a *real* shot."

These words sting my eyes, tears threatening to fall. Maybe my grandmother is right. Sure, I'd grown up in a nice family. I did okay in school. I had friends and never wanted for much. But there is something to be said about being the average middle child sandwiched between two overachievers. My parents often overlooked me, and since my goals were different from those of my siblings, they wrote them off as frivolous.

Scars left by neglect or disappointment can't be seen, but they run so deep that sometimes I feel like a doll who's been mended one time too many.

Is that why I can't seem to keep my feet planted in one place? Why I have to try new thing after new thing, just to find the path that will make me look the most desirable to them?

"They provided for me, they were good to me. I love them." I practically choke on the words.

"Just because you love them doesn't mean they aren't flawed. It doesn't mean they didn't hurt you beyond measure." Grandma nods. "Being a parent is difficult. Nurturing three minds at the same time is tough, and some shoe is bound to drop. But it doesn't mean you can't pick that shoe right up and run toward your dreams with it."

I giggle. "Enough metaphors, Grandma. I get it. Although, what kind of shoe was it? I'm hoping a really expensive pair of heels."

She scoops me up into a hug I didn't volunteer for, but I relax against her. "I think it's no shoes. I think you should do this yoga thing. Kill it, as the young folks say."

"It's not just the studio or you selling your business. The one you've spent a lifetime building, might I add." I look down at my hands.

"Of course it's not. Keaton Nash told you he loves you and you're running like Cinderella turning back into a pumpkin."

My head shoots up, my mouth falling open in shock. "How did you know that?"

"Child, didn't I tell you you're more like me than you ever could have imagined?" She chuckles. "It's written all over your face. You love that boy back but are too damn scared of it to tell him. Or to stay put. You're like a twitchy mouse ready to scurry away."

Finally defeated, and completely giving over to my feelings, my shoulders sag. "What if I screw it all up? What if he, and everyone in this town, realize that I don't measure up to any of it."

Grandma gets up now and takes hold of my hands. "Presley, you might have been the kind of person I described just before, but you're not her anymore. You are the type of woman who comes to help when her grandmother can't take care of herself anymore. You are the type of woman who empowers other women through exercise and positive thinking. You are the type of woman who helps her boyfriend's mother get her house ready for sale. Fawn Hill has changed you, my dear. Now don't be a damn fool and ignore that fact. And don't be a moron when it comes to Keaton Nash. Go tell that boy you love him. It's my dying wish."

My laugh is garbled with unshed tears. "Oh, stop it, you old kook."

Deep down though, her words struck the doubt I'd let linger there for most of my life. She was the person who, for the first time ever, was helping me see just how worthy I was of everything that was coming to me. And I couldn't leave her, not when I knew what she said was true.

I also needed to finally be a fucking adult and pull on my big girl panties.

You know, the ones Dr. Keaton Nash had pulled out of Grandma's dog's butt.

Yeah, it was finally time to show him those, metaphorically, and tell him how I really felt.

## 33

I ring his doorbell before my head can talk my heart out of it.

We haven't seen each other in nearly four days, and that's the longest we've gone since the night he took me to the water tower. After Grandma smacked some sense into my head, I threw my clothes out of the duffel and onto the floor of my room. I could only adult so much at one time and folding and organizing would have to wait.

Because tonight, I was going to tell the first man I'd ever said it to that I loved him.

It takes a few minutes, but I hear the lock being turned and then the door swings inward, revealing Keaton.

In nothing but basketball shorts. God, why did he have to be so freaking handsome? I was going to be insanely distracted during this if he didn't put a shirt on.

"Presley." His eyes go wide, and the tone of his voice holds surprise.

"Hey." I smile sheepishly, holding up a hand.

Keaton looks mildly confused and hasn't said anything else ... and I'm still standing on his front porch after half a minute.

"Can I come in?" I'm suddenly so nervous, I feel like I might throw up.

How does one say I love you to the first person they've ever told it to, in a romantic sense, and not feel like they're jumping out of a plane?

"Yeah, sure." He steps aside, and when I move past him into the landing of his split level, I get a waft of the clean, soapy scent he always sports.

Gosh, I've missed him. The feeling swamps me, and before I know what I'm doing, I wrap my arms around his waist and press my cheek to his bare chest.

At first, Keaton goes still, and I know that I've hurt him. That makes my heart ache because I truly hadn't considered it. While I was busy having a full-on meltdown over this man telling me he loves me, he'd been sitting in his house waiting for me. Or fearing that we were over. I'd left him in radio silence and he'd been his usual upstanding self and given me the space.

"I'm sorry," I apologize to his pec, and finally he relents, wrapping those long, lean arms around me.

Against my hip, his phone starts to ring in his pocket. He reaches a hand down, finding it inside and silencing it.

He moves away from me, his eyes a blazing, deep caramel, and I know he's trying to find the words.

Instead, he says, "Let's have a drink."

Yeah, wine sounded like a good idea for this conversation. I nod and follow him up the stairs to the first level of his house. Once I crest the top stair, his phone starts to go off again.

Keaton pulls it out of his pocket this time, stares at the screen, growls and clicks it off until he goes silent.

"Why do my brothers call at the worst times?" He gives me a small smile.

"Because they love you but are also the annoyance of your existence. At least that's how I feel about my siblings." I shrug.

And now that I think about it, once I confess that I'm in love with him, I want to spend more time getting to know his brothers. I've only hung out with them on a couple of occasions, and those are the people closest to Keaton. I want to become a part of their group ... and I want them to know how I feel about their brother. It's just clicked as a very important thing I need to show them.

"Keaton, I wanted to come over to say—"

My sentence is cut off as his phone rings again.

"Goddammit," he bites out and looks at it once more, then up at me. "I'm sorry."

He clicks the button to answer it and lifts it to his ear, his tone pure annoyance. "What is it?"

I wait as he listens to whoever is on the other end of the phone, his expression growing more grave by the second. He starts to nod and then bites his lip, and while he still has the phone pressed to his ear, he marches to his bedroom and appears back in front of me with a T-shirt covering his once bare chest.

"I'll meet you there in twenty."

He hangs up abruptly and looks at me; his mind somewhere completely different. "That was Bowen. Fletcher is in serious trouble, I have to go."

"Let me come with you!" I call at his back, the thought popping out before I can think.

"If you want to." He doesn't even turn around to look at me when he says it, and I try not to let that sting.

He's just worried about his brother. This has nothing to do with the fact that I didn't say I love you back to him the other night. Or at least I can hope that it doesn't.

Keaton doesn't speak the entire ride, and I don't prod him. I can see the twitch of his jaw, the sharp set of his eyebrows, the way his knuckles turn white as he grips the wheel. My responsible, *good* man is speeding ... something he *never* does. And it's this ... the body language he's radiating across the truck, that has me panicking.

This is going to be bad.

I square my shoulders and take a deep breath, mentally preparing myself to be strong.

We pull onto a dirt road that winds deep between trees on an unlit road. About half a mile down, the forest breaks to reveal a plot of land that contains a broken-down, beat-up shack of a house. The siding must have been white at some point in time, but now it's filthy and moss and leaves grow between the panels. Half the shutters have fallen off, the front porch steps look like they'd cause a broken ankle if stepped on, and there are half-built cars littering the lot. Garbage is scattered around the grassless land, and mud puddles mark the earth like bullet holes.

My heart rate spikes, because I know this isn't the type of home where anything good happens. No ... this is the site of something very bad, and I'm assuming, dangerous.

"Stay in the car," Keaton grits out, his troubled eyes flashing to make sure I'm buckled in.

"Keaton, I don't want you to go in there." Some sixth sense has me wanting him to back down this driveway immediately.

"I'll be fine. Stay here. I mean it, Presley."

I nod, promising with my eyes that I'll stay here. Keaton gets out just as another car pulls up, and I see Bowen meet him in the middle of the dark front yard. They talk quietly and then head up to the house. A flash of metal in Bowen's hand tells me he's holding a gun, and the organ trying to beat out of my chest suddenly jumps into my throat.

They disappear inside, and I'm all too aware that I'm sitting out here alone.

*Fuck staying in the car.* I know Keaton will be furious, but I'm not going to sit back while a person I love is put in danger. I'm done letting life happen to me.

The first thing that hits me is the scent of the air. It's filled with chemicals and almost smells sour. Yelling from inside has me pausing at the front door, my hands shaking as I work up the nerve to push it open.

When I do, I'm hit with a cloud of invisible ... something, and my nostrils flare. The house is more disgusting inside than it is on the outside, and there is no one in a room I'm guessing is supposed to be the living room that I walk into. Quietly, I walk farther in, pausing when I hear what sounds like stomping feet from somewhere within.

Another two rooms passed through, and a voice catches my ear.

"Well, what do we have here?"

I turn to see a man, taller than Keaton but thinner than me, his two gold front teeth gleaming from a wicked, evil smile.

"I'm just looking for my boyfriend and his brothers." I try to stand my ground, but when he advances, my instincts have me stepping back.

Alarm bells are sounding in my head when this man, dirt caked on his clothes and hands, smiles at my retreat.

"Boyfriend, huh? Bet I can show you a better time than he does."

As he comes closer, I can see the red, enflamed blood vessels in his eyes, and the way his arms won't stop twitching and moving. I step back again, not wanting him to invade my space any further, but he isn't stopping. When my back hits the wall, I go to twist away and run down the hall, but his large hand captures my wrist.

"Hey, baby, where you going so fast?" He leers at me.

I bring my other hand up, prepared to hit him and run whichever way I can when someone else beats me to it.

"Get your hands off of her!" Keaton growls, pushing the guy, whose state has him falling over and stumbling into a chair.

"Keaton ..." I start for him, wanting him to catch me in his arms, but he puts a hand up, holding me steady by the shoulder.

"I can't do this with you here." His eyes are stone-cold, angry.

I've disobeyed him and probably made this situation that much worse.

"What the fuck, man?" The creep stands up, and another man I don't recognize walks into the room.

"Do we have a problem here?" This man is cleaner and doesn't seem to be high like his cohort.

"Just came for my brother." Keaton's face is void of expression.

I see Bowen in the background, down the hall, dragging a half-conscious Fletcher by the upper arm.

"Your brother owes me money. And I don't need word of this place getting out. You understand that, right?"

The tone of this man's voice lets us all know that isn't a question ... it's a threat. My blood is ice in my veins. What the hell has Fletcher gotten himself into?

"How much does he owe you?" Keaton grits out between bared teeth.

I've never seen the man I love so incensed. Keaton Nash is a level-headed, kind, amiable doctor. He shouldn't be in a place like this, dealing with people like this. His loyalty to his brother has landed him here, and anyone in the room can feel the fury rolling off of him in waves.

"Three grand." The director of this ... drug house—I don't want to say meth because I know nothing about it—flicks his coat to the side.

I see the flash of the gun at his belt, it's unmistakable.

Keaton calmly pulls out his wallet without taking his eyes off the man. "Here is five hundred dollars. You have my word that

I'll be back tomorrow with the rest. Now we're taking my brother."

Bowen walks past us, Fletcher lolling all over him, as Keaton steps between me and the two strange men. I slip my hand into his, not because I want him to know I'm okay, but because I feel the wrath of what's about to come down over us. These men might not harm us, but I know I just made some mistake. I can feel it. And when he leaves his hand limp instead of curling it around mine that fear is confirmed.

"You better be back tomorrow, Nash. Don't forget that this is a small town, a small county. I know where your mother lives, and I can find out where your pretty redhead here lives, too."

My lungs seize, the air I don't let out burning from within them.

Keaton pulls me toward the door. "You have my word."

# 34

"**I** told you to stay in the car."

I breathe in and out of my nose, trying not to scream at Presley. I'm not even sure I could, with the exhaustion and adrenaline downshift flooding my bones.

My car has long since been shut off, put in park in my driveway, but we haven't gotten out. If we did, I'd have to invite her inside to have this conversation, and I don't know what I want to do yet.

Why had she shown up here tonight? What did she want to talk about before all hell had broken loose?

My God ... Fletcher was messed up with the drug dealers who apparently started a meth house just over the county line. How the hell had he gotten involved in that? I knew his drinking was getting out of control, but this?

I look at the steering wheel of my car as if it will provide answers. I'm not sure if I want to punch it until my hands bleed, collapse my head in my hands and cry, or pray to my father, wherever he is, and ask what the plan is? What do I do? I'm not equipped to help my brother with something as big as getting clean from meth.

And then there is Presley.

Seeing that guy touch her, the gun on their leader's belt and the place I'd taken her to? Having her there was more than I could bear. I'd needed to help my brother, to get him out of there, but I couldn't breathe the moment she'd walked into that hell hole. All I wanted to do was abandon every thought of saving my family, of being the leader of the Nash boys, and carry her the fuck out. Over my shoulder like a caveman.

I'm livid she didn't follow my instructions to stay in the car.

"I know, I'm so sorry. I thought ... I wanted to help ..."

"Well, you didn't help!" My voice is louder and filled with more rage than I wanted to let bleed into it. "You only identified yourself to them. Do you realize how reckless these guys can be? This isn't New York, Presley. There aren't cops keeping real tabs on these guys. They roam the surrounding areas praying on the weak and for the most part, going unchecked. And now they know your face."

She has the decency to drop her eyes in shame. "I couldn't let anything happen to you."

And in her recklessness, she'd let everything happen to me. When that creep had put his hands on her, I'd seen my life flash before my eyes. I was in too deep, with a woman who had no regard for her well-being or the feelings I'd confessed to her. Feelings she hadn't returned.

"I think we should ... take some time." The words feel like sawdust in my mouth.

"What ... what are you saying?" Presley's voice notches up an emotional octave.

My right hand scrubs over my face. I haven't been able to process anything that has happened in the last three hours, my brain is fried, my emotions are all over the place and I know I'm going to fuck this up but I don't care.

"I've dedicated a lot of time to you in the past couple of

months. And I've really enjoyed it ... but I have a life here. I have people I need to take care of. You ... you make that complicated."

"So, you're saying, that because of who I am, because of how I affect you, you want to end this? You're telling me that you feel too deeply about me, and I'm reckless, and it's dangerous because it makes you stray from your same-old routine? Well, excuse me for bringing a little spontaneity to your life. Excuse me for trying to better you as a person."

Her words sting.

"Oh, come on, Presley. I saw you the other night when I told you I was in love with you. You looked like you were about to sprout wings and fly into the atmosphere. Anything to get away from me as fast as you possibly could. I told you how I felt about you and you avoided me for almost an entire week. Don't tell me this was moving at the speed you wanted it to. You're so freaked out about how we feel about each other that you can't even say it back, let alone be around me. From the very start, you had no intention of putting down roots here. I think ... I think this is going to be best for both of us. I think we both knew from the beginning that we were too different to ever work. You said it on our first date. That you didn't know if you could see us together. If we're being honest, this"—I point back and forth between us —"might have been dead on arrival. Maybe it's good that it's ending before either of us get seriously hurt."

My words are lies, burning their way out of my throat. I was *already* seriously hurt. My heart had been broken the second she hadn't returned the feelings I'd told her about. But there was no point damaging my ego, and my pride, even further. Closing myself off would have to do.

Is this why Katie had just left all of those years ago instead of breaking up with me in person? Because it was easier than having the conversation, than cutting yourself open and bleeding and then trying to stitch it all back up. How I wished I could do that instead of sitting here being a full-on masochist in front of a green-eyed beauty.

"That's really how you feel?" I can hear the tears in her throat, see the sparkle of them out of the corner of my eye as they roll down her cheeks.

But I refuse to look at her. I only nod.

"Okay, then. If that's what you want. We're done."

Her words aren't mad or angry. They're worse. They're final. Empty and hollow.

As soon as they leave her mouth, she's opening the passenger door and fleeing into the night. I almost want to get out, to make sure no one follows her home, but that would be hypocritical.

I didn't have to worry about her anymore. We were over.

And out of everything that had happened tonight, our demise was the thing cracking my heart into icy, bleeding shards.

## 35

He'd dumped me and I didn't even have the courage to tell him that I was going to stay in Fawn Hill.

I'd been too much of a wimp to tell him that I was going to buy the space for the yoga studio.

And worst of all, I was far too scared to tell him that I love him back when he accused me of running.

Part of the reason Keaton had ended things between us was because I'd been his weakness. His distraction that kept him from fulfilling all the duties of his life. To know that I was the thing that made him reckless that threw his schedule off balance ... shame wasn't a big enough word to describe what I felt.

Keaton Nash was nothing if not a stand-up, responsible, in-charge kind of guy. He thrived on order, and I'd thrown his life into chaos. My personality, my instincts, the way he blew off his normal life to be with me instead ... it devastated me that I was the cause of his turmoil.

And to know that Fletcher could have ended up in much worse shape if Keaton hadn't ignored that third phone call ... God, it killed me. My heart physically hurt knowing that just another second wasted, and he could have been gone.

Keaton's words had hurt, like a burn branding my shame with each syllable. The things he'd said about me being freaked out, about me not wanting to stick around, about our relationship being dead on arrival ... they stung so badly because they were true.

But I was at fault too for the way my heart felt now. Like the skin had been flayed off. As if it were a dead machine rotting for spare parts inside my body. The ache I'd been rubbing at in the middle of my breastbone all week was the cause of a spark of joy, of hope for a future, being fully stamped out.

I'd gone to Keaton's house that night with the intention of telling him that I love him. That I am in love with him. And within a couple of hours, the fire that Grandma had lit under me to tell him how I felt had been completely extinguished.

My heart was broken. What he'd said to me, that we'd been "dead on arrival"? I could feel the lashings he'd doled out on it.

Like everything else in my life, maybe my romance with Keaton was fleeting. All the things that happened to me only lasted for a very short time. I glimpsed happiness or success, and then it was gone. A wisp of a dream, a shooting star gone too soon.

I'd been moping around the store for the last week, slinking behind the alley to walk or drive home a route that took double the time than if I just headed down Main Street. But that would put me in a direct path to spot the vet's office. And then I'd slow down, press my foot to the brakes, just to see if I could catch a glimpse of Keaton.

And that was pathetic. So I was instead, like the mature adult that I was, driving double the time and avoiding the places I knew he'd be.

In better news, I wasn't running scared. The man I love may have broken up with me and called me reckless, but I was trying to be far from that. Because I may not be creating a love life in Fawn Hill, but I sure as hell was building a life. I'd decided to stay, and the first act to furthering that was telling Grandma to put the bookshop on the market.

It had stunned a lot of residents when she'd done it, and we both knew they were gossiping about the two of us and my involvement with her giving up the store. None of them knew what we were planning ... well, except for Jerica Tenny, the realtor who was helping me look at commercial listings for the yoga studio I wanted to open up.

Jerica was a slim, short woman probably around the age of my mom, except she looked nothing like the realtors I'd dealt with in New York City. She was the kind of motherly figure who looked like she baked pies and sewed costumes, instead of being the real estate maven of Fawn Hill. Which I mean, probably wasn't as demanding as the city, but Jerica was whip smart and fair. I actually really liked her.

"This space just dropped in price because the buyer who bought the building was going to convert it, but the idea never passed the town planning committee. So, it's within your budget, and I could probably get them to come down a bit so that you'd have enough to get a loan to fix the space as you want it."

Jerica led Grandma and me around the half-finished space. I watched my footing, carefully trying not to step on nails or piles of sawdust. The ceiling was ... non-existent, and some of the walls were half-installed. It needed paint, hardwood, an outfitted front desk space, a locker room, cubbies ...

*But.* It was the first location she'd taken us to see that had floor-to-ceiling windows on two sides. The natural light in here was off the charts. And if I was forced to teach inside rather than in the park, I'd take all the natural light I could get. The shape of the space was also ideal, I could almost envision where everything would go. And it was within the budget Grandma and I had painstakingly gone over.

"Under budget would be good. This place needs a good spit shine." Grandma nodded her head.

I'd been taking some basic online business courses at night because if I was going to do this, it was time to buckle down. I'd learn about basic accounting, bookkeeping, customer support, marketing, and all the other things that no one realized went into owning a business. It was overwhelming, yes, but for the first time in my life, I was truly excited about my professional goals.

Looking out the window, I noticed it had another perk. It was located just off the core set of shops on Main Street, on the side toward Grandma's house. Which meant I wouldn't have to drive past the vet's office.

Jerica and Grandma were staring at me now. I knew that they saw right through into my thoughts. A blush creeps across my cheeks. I'm not embarrassed that Grandma knows my heartbreak.

It's that the entire town knows Keaton dumped me that's causing the shame. People I don't even know whisper about me on the street. I can feel their eyes track me as I workout in the park or pick up dinner from Kip's to take home for Grandma and me. Were they calling me desperate? Did it look strange that an outsider would stay in Fawn Hill after their boy wonder kicked her to the curb?

I try to push the sadness and those shameful thoughts from my mind.

"I think this is the one," I say with more confidence than I feel.

Because I love the space, and I love my idea, but what do I know about starting a business? Virtually nothing. I have a feeling I'll be getting a crash course as soon as the keys to this place are in my hands.

Jerica smiles, and Grandma winks at me. "I'll start drawing up the papers."

We all take a collective breath as we get back into the car, an uncomfortable, sorrowful silence washing over us.

"If that wasn't the hardest thing I've ever had to do." Mom's voice breaks, and even though she's in the back seat, I know she's dissolved into a puddle of tears.

My eyes shoot to the rearview, where I see Forrest take her in his arms, letting her cry into his shirt. His eyes are bloodshot, and still in a stupor of shock. He wasn't with Bowen and me last week when we'd saved his twin brother from a meth house and then paid off his debts. For a long time, I think Forrest has wanted to turn a blind eye to Fletcher's addiction because he loves him, and because it's easier not to stir up trouble.

Honestly, we've all done it. But after the dangerous position he got himself in ... Bowen and I knew we couldn't allow this to keep going. No more seeing if he could pull it together, no more homegrown interventions. Our brother needs help, and now, he'll get it.

The sign on the building looms over the hood of my car. Calyard's Clinic. The name masks what actually goes on inside the nice exterior. Drug treatment, detoxing, therapy for addicts, recovery and sober-living education. Fletcher had kicked and screamed when we'd told him two days ago that we were bringing him in. It was only when Mom stepped in, her voice flat and low as a stone pummeled by a river, that he listened. She told him his father was watching that he was disgracing the man who gave him his name. She told him she would not stand by and watch him kill himself. I feel like I've swallowed glass just thinking of that moment.

Besides the day my dad died ... today was the lowest day I could ever remember for our family.

We'd all gone to check Fletcher in, with Bowen and I now sitting in the front seat of my car, and Forrest and Mom in the back. We felt incomplete; this wasn't our family unit. We weren't united. And we wouldn't be for another three months. Fletcher was going for a strict ninety days, and even though he could check himself out, I knew he wouldn't.

I'd seen his face, I'd been the last one to leave his room. He looked like the little boy I remember helping up after he scraped his knee for the first time. Scared, frightened, in pain ... but also a little invincible. Like the world could throw anything at him and he'd still rise again to fight another day.

I hope to God he gets healthy and sober.

"He's going to do it, Ma. I just know it." Forrest tries to comfort Mom as I put the car in reverse and then drive, steering us toward home.

It takes us forty minutes to get back to Mom's house, which is pretty much empty at this point. Everything has been packed into boxes or sold, and we're doing a final moving day next weekend to help get her settled in her townhouse. She chose a newer construction home in the section of town that has gone through a development boom in the last two years.

I told her she could move in with one of us and not rent until she found something she loved, but she refused. Said she didn't want to infringe on us. Really, I think she's just anxious to start the next chapter of her life. With the house sold and her husband gone, I think Mom is looking to take a couple of deep breaths and start anew as best as she can.

Forrest sits down at the kitchen island. "This is so weird. This whole day, just … strange."

Bowen harrumphs in agreement, walking to the set of windows that looks out onto the backyard.

"I wish Dad were here." The quiet words come out of my mouth before I can even stop them.

My brothers look at me, stunned. Bowen speaks first. "I do, too. I bet he's happy she's sold it."

Forrest looks down at his hands. "He would have done that stupid wink and then told her he was proud."

From the doorway, a sob rings out. We all turn swiftly, to see Mom standing there, tears streaming down her face.

"Thank you. Thank all of you. We raised you boys right, we raised you to be the best kind of men. Your father … he would have been proud of all of us."

I go to her because I'm the oldest. I'm the one who carries the team now, who picks us up when we're down.

Mom's back heaves up and down as I pat it, as the wetness from her eyes soaks into my shirt. I blink up, trying not to get emotional. I don't know that I have anything left in me. Between talking about Dad, where we dropped Fletcher off at today, and Presley …

She sniffles, gulping hard as she straightens to look at me. Her dark eyes narrow, the same color as my own. "And he'd want you to do the same. Move on, I mean. I see the way you look at Presley. Don't be a fool, Keaton. Tell that girl you love her that you can't live without her."

"This isn't about me." I huff, turning away.

"Oh, yes, it is. And while it's my turn to get real with you, I need you to know that you're not responsible for everyone else's problems. Your brothers can make their own mistakes and learn to clean them up. You're not their keeper, and you shouldn't be expected to be mine. You have to live, too, sweetheart."

Her words hit the most vulnerable spot inside of me, the one that prickles with shame and aches from being broken. Since my father died ...

Hell, even before that. I've always felt this sense of responsibility. Do everything in an orderly fashion. Family over everything. Duty over happiness. Love should only happen in a practical, ducks-in-a-row kind of a way. Date, get engaged, get married, buy a house, have kids.

But ... my life was living proof that nothing ever happened according to plan. And here I was, still trying to control it and live by these ridiculous ideals I'd set up for myself.

"She was only trying to protect you that night, Keat." Bowen's expression tells me he's on Mom's side.

"She's reckless. She ... she, she makes me act spontaneously. I'm not a child. I'm a man with a business and responsibilities."

"And I'd say the fact that she just purchased a storefront on Main Street says that she's just as serious about making a life here as you are." Forrest is looking down at his phone.

Mom clucks her tongue at him.

He shrugs. "What? Accessing building records and real estate deals is like, the easiest thing ever."

Presley had bought a storefront? Obviously, I knew that Hattie had put the book shop up for sale but ...

She was really putting down roots in Fawn Hill. Despite my rejection, despite my idiocy in letting her go, she was making a decision to settle in.

And just like that, my heart started beating again.

"I told her I loved her and she didn't say it back," I tell them all for the first time.

Before right now, no one knew the secret pain I'd been hiding. Her unwillingness to give me those emotions back burned in the deepest chambers of my heart.

Bowen's voice is quiet when he speaks. "You can love someone very much and not be able to say it."

No one touches that with a ten-foot pole. Instead, Mom turns back to me and takes my face in her hands.

"Your father told me he loved me on our second date. We'd known each other for ten days, and he professed his love to me. To say I was shocked would be an understatement. It took me an entire month after that to say it back. You are so much like him it scares me sometimes. Keaton, you are a man who knows exactly what you want. You say how you feel when you feel it. You're humble, intelligent, loyal and when you love someone, they know it. You're the best kind of person. But ... you can also be a bit intimidating. Presley loves you, I know that girl does, but she just needs some time to sort out her feelings. She chose you because you're the type of man who will let her. Who will still be waiting there for her when she does finally come to that conclusion. And if she needs a little push, because she is who she is, then you give her a little push. Be her steadiness, be her patience. And when you can't be that anymore, put it all on the line."

"Grand freaking gesture, man," Forrest echoes our mother.

Mom's words open my eyes to the thing I haven't been able to see all along. The one that's been right in front of me.

Presley and I ... we chose each other *because* of our differences, not in spite of them. I love that she forces me to be spontaneous, and I think she loves that I ground her.

"But I ended things."

Mom waves me off. "Please, as if men don't do stupid things

all the time. I raised four boys, I should know. You go to her and make things right. Or would you rather be alone and heart-broken forever?"

"Jeez, way to be harsh, Ma." Forrest chuckles.

She was right. I knew that. I'd known it since the moment I'd acted like an idiot and let go of the one woman I'd ever truly loved.

But, Presley was staying in Fawn Hill, which sparked a tiny flicker of hope in my chest.

Maybe I had one last shot.

The sale of the storefront at the end of Main Street hasn't gone through yet, but that doesn't keep me from visiting it every morning.

With coffee in hand, I stand across the street, staring at the empty windows and half-done space beyond them ... just dreaming of what this place will look like a year from now. *My place.*

Well, technically, it's almost all Grandma's ... but it's my dream and I can lay claim to that.

I can see the shiny, light wooden floors with yoga mats unrolled all over them. I can see the wall of mirrors I'll install on the entire back of the space. I'll call some of my friends from the city, see if they can get me some merchandise shipped down here that I could sell. The whole studio will have a relaxed, homey vibe and it will be a peaceful space for Fawn Hill to not only get their bodies in shape but their minds, too.

I've already told Lily and Penelope about it, and, of course, those two then told everyone else. I've gotten phone calls and passerby conversations about how excited the women who already take my class in the park are.

The sale of the bookshop, and the acquisition of this space plus the courses I've been taking and the contractors I've been interviewing ... it has all kept my mind off of Keaton.

Sort of. Okay, not really, but a girl can use denial as a tool and a shield, right?

I take a sip of coffee, loving the bitter but energizing bite of it, and turn my head to look at the bustle of Main Street in the morning. Fawn Hill may be a small town, but its citizens are grinders. They're up before dawn tending their farms, they're loyally ordering their coffee from Java, they're mailing their packages and dropping their kids off at school or opening their own businesses' doors to welcome in other residents. I like that the studio is at the end of the block, that I can observe the morning busyness from afar, but still catch a glimpse of it. It'll remind me who I'm doing this for.

I'm scanning the crowd running their morning errands down the street, so I don't catch his face separating from the rest of the townspeople until it's too late and awkward to just walk off.

"Hi." Keaton walks toward me, a coffee in his hand as well.

My heart picks up the pace, while my brain tries to tell the stupid, foolish thing to quit it. *He dumped us, remember?*

"Hi." I nod politely and sip my coffee, turning my head so that I'm looking at my future studio and not the man who broke my heart.

He stands next to me, looking like the definition of fall in his worn-in blue jeans and cream cable-knit sweater. He looks cozy and warm, and I have the sudden urge to be wrapped up all day in him like a good blanket. I have to physically restrain myself from moving closer.

"How have you been?" Keaton's voice is tender, and I wonder why he's even over here.

Has he been watching me watch the studio each morning?

Does he think about me anymore? It's only been about two weeks since he ended things on that horrible night we saved Fletcher, but it feels like an eternity.

I look down at my feet out of habit. "I've been good, thanks."

This conversation is awkward and stifled ... and strange. Strange because even when we first met, even when I turned him down the first, and second, time, Keaton and I have always known how to banter. We've always been able to be honest in talking to one another. And now, I'm just straight up lying.

I can see his head bobbing up and down in a nod. "I heard through the grapevine that you bought this place."

A small smile breaks my frown. "You can never do anything in this town without everyone knowing."

"No, you cannot." Keaton takes a sip of coffee. "So, a yoga studio? That's what you're going to turn it into, right?"

"Yes." I don't feel like being here.

Talking to him is painful, doesn't he know that? Well ... maybe he doesn't. I never told him how I felt. He ended it before I could.

But as much as I want to be angry with him, I can't. As much as I want to accuse him of ruining things between us, yell at him and demand to know why he sought me out ... I won't. I know why he ended things. Keaton Nash is the most responsible man I know. He has so much on his plate that he can't make room for a woman who is so indecisive about her feelings and her future.

Keaton turns so that he's standing in front of me, not next to me like before, and I'm forced to look at him. His facial hair is scruffier than usual, and although he's as gorgeous as ever, his eyes hold exhaustion. I'd heard through that ever-present town grapevine that the Nash family had taken Fletcher to rehab, and I know how hard this must be for Keaton. He'll look at it as his own personal failure.

"You're going to do so great. I'm really proud of you, Presley. You're following your dreams, and that is amazing."

Keaton looks like he wants to say something more, and his hand raises as if he's about to run it through my hair. Just like he did every morning we were together. As if his fingers connecting with my locks was just as soothing for him as it was for me.

I'm waiting with bated breath, because I can feel the hope sparking between us. It's building in the air, and I want so badly to reach out and grab it, spin it into something that's tangible and real that I can give to both of us.

"I only ever started on this journey because of you. You made me believe in myself," I whisper, my eyes searching his.

*Tell him you love him.*

It's on the tip of my tongue, but Keaton cuts me off.

"You had it in you all along. I just reminded you of what you could be. Good luck, Presley. You're going to be incredible."

And then he turns on his heel and slowly walks off, shaking his head.

I'm left standing in front of my future studio, wondering what the hell just happened?

A nd, nerdy, fumbling Keaton Nash was back.

Remember him? The guy who couldn't get Presley McDaniel to agree to a date until the third time he asked. And even then, she rejected me at the end of it.

I thought I'd been charming, if not a little nervous, in those early encounters. And then I'd won her heart, so, of course, she knew me. Knew how I operated.

But apparently, I'd forgotten all of my slick moves in the three weeks we'd been broken up. I'd forgotten that I had enough game to win her over the first time around. That's why I'd completely crashed and burned, and chickened out, in front of her future yoga studio a couple of days ago.

It took a pep talk in my bathroom mirror before I was able to walk down to the Pumpkin Festival around six p.m. Thank God, Mom didn't wrangle us into a booth for this carnival. Even though caramel corn would be a lot easier to make in the fifty-five-degree weather tonight, rather than the almost ninety in the summer that threatened to sweat our balls off.

But I had the night off, and I knew a certain gorgeous redhead didn't, which worked to my advantage. Through the trusty Fawn Hill gossip line, I'd learned that Presley would be helping Lily at the library's used book stand tonight at the festival. Since I could pin down her whereabouts, and had finally gotten up the balls to tell her how foolish I was for letting her go, I was going with plan B.

Or Forrest's plan, as he was bragging about it earlier.

The grand gesture.

I head straight for the library tent, which is always in the same place in the lineup of businesses advertising in Bloomsbury Park at this festival. The air smells like cinnamon and apples, and the colors of fall are draped over every possible surface.

Lily spots me first, smiling as I approach. "Are you here to buy or sell?"

I look past her, waiting for Presley to turn around and see me. Her long scarlet hair falls in curls down her back where a gray sweater dress wraps around her curves. The swell of her ass, the skin on her bare legs ... they're distracting. But I keep my eyes up, my head straight. I'm on a mission.

"Neither. I'm here for a Ferris wheel ride."

At my voice, Presley's back straightens, and she turns, her green eyes wide.

She doesn't speak, so I ask again, holding my hand out. "What do you say? Join me?"

"I-I'm working here," she stutters.

Lily jumps in. "No, I've got it. You go take a break, you're due anyway."

"I got here half an hour ago." Presley scowls at her.

"It's not even busy! I can handle it. You go have fun." Lily practically pushes her out of the booth.

Once she's standing out in the grass with me, stripped of her duties, the nervous energy sparks between us.

"Shall we?" I start to lead the way and breathe a sigh of relief when she follows.

We climb into the Ferris wheel car, and I have to focus on the fact that I have her in this death trap for the next twenty or so minutes, completely alone. I have to say what I need to say.

The bar closes over our laps, and déjà vu moves in swiftly. It might not be the exact same Ferris wheel, but it's in the exact same spot in Bloomsbury Park, and my jean-clad leg is touching hers, and the nervous energy flowing through my veins almost matches that of the first time she agreed to go on a date with me.

"So, you wanted to take me up here?" Presley looks at me as the car rises.

I dive right in. "I chickened out the other day on Main Street."

Confusion marks her expression. "What?"

"I was coming over to tell you that ... I was an idiot. I was selfish. I was hurt and confused and just wanted it all to stop so I took the easy way out by ending us. But, you need to know. I love you. More than any of the other things that consume my life. I was a coward and a moron, I should have never let you go. I should have told you I'd be here, that I'd wait while you figured your feelings out, instead of running like a scared boy. I'm ready to be the man you can count on. I'm in love with you, Presley."

We stop at the exact peak of the wheel, and I internally high-five myself for having the foresight to slip the teenage ride operator twenty bucks yesterday. I needed to manufacture a little bit of this, just to make sure it went perfectly.

It wasn't every day you needed to grovel for the love of your life.

She sucks in a gasp, and I want so badly to touch her, but I know I have to give her a minute.

"I knocked on your front door that night fully intending to

tell you that I was in love with you." Presley's green eyes are open, vulnerable.

Shock pulses through me. "You were? Wait ... you love me."

She gulps, and I watch her elegant neck during the motion. "I love you, Keaton. I know I had to work up the courage then, just like I do now. I'm so sure of it, and yet I'm scared out of my mind. I've never loved someone this much. Loved someone with so much of me that I'm fighting my instinct to run with every fiber of my being."

"I don't want to change you." I lace my fingers through hers.

Because truly, I don't. If staying here, with me, for me, is that painful for her ... I'll break my own heart again to set her free.

"Well, see, that's how I felt in that moment at your front door. I was fighting that instinct. But now, I barely feel it at all. You ended things, and that gave me the clarity to see that this is the place I belong. With or without you, Fawn Hill is my home."

Something else clears from the fog in my brain that took over when she said she was in love with me.

"You were coming to tell me you loved me, and I ended things."

Presley looks away, out over the setting sun on the horizon, and nods. When she looks back at me, a single tear escapes her eye.

Instantly, I pull her into my arms. "Oh, God, I'm so sorry. I ... I freaked out. Everything with Fletcher, it overwhelmed me. I hadn't heard from you in days, after telling you how I felt, and my responsibility to my family ... it all was too much in that moment. I thought I had to be a certain way. My entire life, I've felt like I have to be a certain way."

She pulls back, a half-laugh half-sob coming out of her mouth. "And that's one of the reasons you're such a good man. Why I love you."

I cut her off, just because I need to get this out. "But you came along and threw my straight and narrow out the window. And thank God you did. You showed me that life doesn't have to be black and white, it can be shades of gray, or better, shades of color. We can go off script and still accomplish goals and be there for the people counting on us ... honestly, it makes life that much sweeter. You taught me that. I was too afraid to see it, too scared of throwing away the rule book, but I'm not now. I have you."

Presley kisses me first, practically jumps in my lap and sends the car teetering dangerously back and forth. I wrap my arms around her, threading my fingers in her hair because I've missed that feeling so much. Her mouth consumes mine, and I pour everything I have into my own kiss to her.

My apologies.

My love.

My excitement for a future with her.

As we exit the ride, we do it hand in hand. We're connected, our past left somewhere at the top of the wheel.

There is only the great, wonderful future ahead of us.

## 39

We wake on and off throughout the night; the sheets cocooning our bodies, our hands wandering.

Our fingers are drunk with sleep, but the haze of lust is more powerful, and won't let us slip back under until we've satisfied each other. Keaton's sighs tingle down my frame, leaving goose bumps in their wake. My eyes aren't even open, I'm with him only by touch and sound.

"I love you," he murmurs in my ear as he rolls on top of me, slipping into me.

I bury my face in his neck, inhaling the scent of his skin as he slowly rolls in and out of me. "I love you so much."

He makes love to me softly, slowly, achingly. The warmth of his skin seeps into mine, our moans mingle until they are one. Keaton stokes my desire, leaving me burning long after I climax. He follows on my orgasm's heels, growling quietly as his tongue assaults my mouth, his cock pulsing inside me.

I'm not sure what time it is when the light finally reaches behind my lids and has me blinking out of my sleep. Keaton is still in the bed beside me, which is rare for him, because he's usually an up-at-dawn kind of person. It gives me a chance to observe him, to trace the lines of his body and face with my eyes, while he's this vulnerable and peaceful.

When I went to work the Pumpkin Festival with Lily last night, ending it on the Ferris wheel telling Keaton I loved him was the last thing I thought would happen. Obviously, I'm incredibly elated that it did, but this all still feels pretty surreal.

One minute, I was in denial about nursing a severely damaged heart, and the next, my real life dream man was kissing me back after I took a chance and attacked his mouth.

But, that's how Keaton has always been with me. Honest, open, and he has no qualms about how serious he is about a future with me. That's what I wanted to show him, how I wanted to tell him about my feelings. Up on that Ferris wheel, I meant it when I said I wasn't scared, that I had no urge to flee at the first sign of commitment anymore.

That's how much I love him.

Now, his chest rises and falls in time with his sleep-breathing, and I admire the curve of his bicep where it's tossed over my waist. His eyelashes fan his cheeks, and there is a little bit of drool on his pillow.

Mr. Perfect isn't entirely perfect, after all.

Except ... he is.

My stomach growls, *loudly*, and I try to shrug away from him as to not disturb his beauty sleep. But Keaton stirs, smiling as he pulls me back to him, and I bury my head in the warmth of his chest.

"Hungry, huh?" He chuckles, rubbing his big hands up and down my back.

"Someone left me famished throughout the night." I giggle as his hands roam to my hips, squeezing the ticklish spot.

"Hmm, I could whip us up something." He makes no move to get out of bed.

"Can you make Shirley Temple eggs? I've been craving them and no one makes them like you."

As I say it, my mouth waters. Thank God I found a man who can cook, 'cause lord knows I can burn the water in a spaghetti pot without even trying.

"That I can do ... if you weren't so distracting." Keaton flips me over, laying on top of me as his hands frame my face.

He's about to kiss me ... when my stomach makes the most horrific gurgle I've ever heard. We both crack up, and he sits up on his knees, maneuvering out of bed.

"All right, all right ... I get it. Breakfast first, then sex. Guess your stomach is dictating what happens this morning." He laughs as he pads into the bathroom.

My feet hit the floor and I walk across the bedroom that I've missed so much. Going to his dresser, I pick out one of the worn, soft T-shirts that I love to wear as a nightgown.

And I know that when we do make it down to the kitchen, I'll sit on the middle stool at his counter as I watch him cook, sipping a cup of coffee.

It's our routine. Our boring, same day-in and day-out schedule that we've created since we got together. And I love it.

Look at me, learning to settle down and commit. And what's more, absolutely loving the life that had always meant to find me.

## 40

The grill flames lick into the sky, the scent of spices and meat and the last of the summer vegetables mingling in the air.

"Are we sure we trust him to cook us dinner?" Forrest points at me using his beer bottle.

"I'm the best cook out of any of you, just ask Mom," I shoot back.

Mom holds her hands up from where she sits next to Presley on the patio couch. "I will not vote in this matter. I love you all equally."

Forrest snorts. "Yeah, right."

"Presley?" I ask my girlfriend.

She tilts her head. "Well, I do love you. But ... I haven't tasted your brothers' cooking."

"Traitor." I give her a stink-eye.

I'm about to ask her who gave her an orgasm this morning and did she want more of those ... and then I remember that my mother is sitting beside her and clamp my lips shut.

We're all gathered in my backyard on the first day of October. It's kind of a celebration of the end of summer months, with the cool breeze blowing through our hair and the fire pit spitting flames nearby. It's also an excuse to all get together, not that we don't see each other almost every day. But now that Presley is part of our circle, Mom will use any fake holiday to get all of her children together.

Well, *almost* all of her children.

It's been about three weeks since Fletcher went to the rehabilitation center, and he's doing well. We all try to call once a week, if he's allowed phone calls at the times we call, to talk about his progress and just to take his mind off of how hard the road ahead is going to be. When I do talk to him, he sounds clearer than I've heard him in a very long time. I pray to whoever is up there that he'll be just as successful when he gets out of there.

"Hey, do you think the Pirates are going to win the wild card?" Bowen asks as he walks out of the sliding doors into the backyard, carrying a bunch of condiments and sides on a tray.

I shrug. "I hope they do."

"Would be a hell of a fun ride to the World Series." He nods, setting the table.

"Forrest, help your brother set the table," Mom instructs our youngest brother.

"I'll help do the dishes," he lies through his teeth.

Presley snorts. "That's what you always say."

We all start cracking up as Forrest scowls at my girlfriend. "How do you know what I've always done? You've only been around full time for a short time, don't start getting cocky on me, Pres."

Usually, I would smack my brother upside the head for talking to my woman like that, but Presley can handle herself. I chuckle at the verbal beat down that is inevitably coming as I use the spatula to put the meat I'm cooking on a serving platter.

"Excuse me, Forrest James, I know that's what you've always

done because I've watched you do it on five different dinner, lunch, or breakfast occasions. You promise you'll clean after everyone cooks and prepares, and magically, you're nowhere to be found when the crap lands in the sink! Sooo, I know you've done it your whole life because people are creatures of habits. Who also form those habits because their family and friends allow them to get away with it. But that's not the case tonight. I'll make sure you clean those dishes if it means stapling your stomach to the counter and cabinets."

We all stare at Presley, slack-jawed, until Mom starts clapping her hands and laughing so hard that tears spring forth from her eyes.

"My God, girl, I knew I loved you." Mom hugs Presley.

Presley just stares at Forrest with a smug, victorious look on her face, and my most egotistical brother seems to cower in fear.

I knew I loved her, too, even before she gave Forrest a total dressing down. That's why I'm going to convince her to move in with me. Not that she knows that yet. But I'm going to do it so subtly, she'll think it's her idea. How smart am I? First I got her to fall in love with me, and now I'm going to trick her into spending the rest of her life with me.

I'm a lucky, lucky man and I know that. Before Presley blew into town, I thought happiness was just a mild feeling. That the life I was living was decent and I shouldn't strive for more.

How wrong I'd been.

Mom, Forrest, and Bowen begin to take their seats around the table while I finish off the rest of the main course on the grill. As I slide the last burger onto the plate, I feel arms wrap around my waist, and catch a lock of fiery hair blowing in the wind out of the corner of my eye.

"I think I should get you one of those aprons that says Kiss the Cook," Presley jokes, nuzzling her cheek to my sweater-clad shoulder.

"You don't need the apron, I'm yours. You can kiss me anytime you want." I look back at her over my shoulder.

"Even in front of your family?" She raises an eyebrow.

I shrug. "My brothers may taunt us, but they're just jealous. Go ahead, lay one on me, gorgeous."

So she does. Plants one on my lips with a searing, hot, quick kiss. And just like I predicted, my brothers begin to heckle us while my mom tries to admonish them.

The smile that traces my mouth and transfers to Presley's is genuine, and I give her lips one more gentle brush before we move to join the taunters for dinner.

And as I look around the table, my family chatting away under the stars, I know that this was the life I was waiting for.

She was the woman I was waiting for.

# EPILOGUE
PRESLEY

**Eight Months Later**

"Thank you all so much for coming today. This was a lifelong dream that I never realized I had until I moved to Fawn Hill. The people here, they've become my family and welcomed me in so loving of a way that I only had the courage to open this studio because of them."

The small crowd gathered on the shiny hardwood of my brand new yoga studio are all faces who have helped get me to this place. A soft open for my brand-new business venture, featuring the people in Fawn Hill I love the most. Grandma, in her jeans and boots ... I knew she wouldn't be open to the free class I was giving for my most valued customers, but she was here and that's what mattered. She'd believed in me when no one else had ... and after all, the business was half hers.

Lily and Penelope, and a couple of my other park yoga regulars who had helped with the concept and design of the studio. I'd made lifelong friends from the moment I'd started to develop this dream, and I'd never be able to put into words how much they meant.

The entire Nash family is here, and they had become my family, too. They had helped with the construction on the studio ... but no one more than Fletcher. While Keaton helped with every spare second he had, he wasn't always available. And once Fletch had gotten out of rehab, he needed something to occupy his time.

We'd grown close, and I'd learned he had much the same feelings about his place in the family as I had with my own brother and sister. Not that it was my place to share that with my boyfriend, but I knew when he felt comfortable enough, Fletcher would open up.

Fletcher stands next to his mother, escorting her around as if she's breakable. He's run to get whatever she needs, and I think he's just so grateful to her for what she helped him through that he feels he owes her, and his brothers, a debt he'll never be able to repay. Which only compounds his feelings of inadequacy. He's been sober for almost nine months, not that there haven't been some almost falls off the wagon.

Keaton stands at my side, a look of pride beaming from his face. I know I never could have done this without him. Even when he had no idea who I really was, had no idea how much I loved the practice of yoga, he'd believed in me enough to suggest going to the library and starting a class in the park.

From the moment I met him, he had done nothing but support and uplift me. He's shown me the side of myself I'd always been searching for, and in doing so, made me fall in love with him.

I'd moved in almost immediately after the Pumpkin Festival, and it had been going well so far. Besides my messy tendencies and some of the late nights Keaton had to work, we'd been crushing the whole living together thing. Ryan had even come to stay with us for a long weekend, and she approved not only of Keaton, but of Fawn Hill. I had a feeling she'd be back soon.

"Do you mind if I say a couple of words in your honor?" He leans over to me, squeezing my hand.

I shake my head, pleasantly surprised. "Not at all."

Not that I expected anyone to say anything, but I'll take praise if my man is willing to give it.

Keaton steps forward, waving to the small crowd and then turning to me. His eyes, the ones I've memorized in every state of emotion, lock on me, a warm smile marking them now.

"I didn't want to overshadow your day, but I didn't know the next time we'd have everyone we cared most about all together in one room, and I couldn't resist telling you how much I love you for all of our friends and family to hear."

My hands begin to shake because you don't say a sentence like that if it isn't pre-empting something monumental. I feel the tears already gathering in the corners of my eyes, and he hasn't even asked the question I know will eventually pop out of his mouth. We haven't talked about this, not in a real sense.

But leave it to the man I taught spontaneity to deliver a surprise I never saw coming.

"Presley, you came into my life at a time when I wasn't sure my path would ever be any different. You turned that thinking, and my world, upside down. You made me fall in love with you from the very first moment even if neither of us could recognize that until later. You're everything that is good, wild and pure about this life. And I can't think of anyone I'd rather walk through it with. I love you … so much that I can't believe sometimes that I'm the one you chose to love back. But you do, and I am never going to take that for granted. So, with that being said …"

Keaton pulls a velvet box from his pocket, holding it up as an offering. When he opens it up, I gasp. A sharp, hot breath sticks in my lungs … because my God does this man know me.

The ring is a gleaming opal surrounded by a halo of

diamonds. It is the shape of a flower, and it's so unique that my knees buckle. I love a good piece of jewelry, but this ring means more than that. Keaton knows me so well that he knows I don't want a regular diamond engagement ring. He loves me and sees the differences inside of me ... this ring translates those and tells them to the world.

"Keaton, oh my—" Now the tears really do start to fall.

"Presley, will you marry me?"

His question is simple, no more declarations. It's no-nonsense, straight-forward, and real. Just like the man that I love.

"Yes. *Yes*." I nod emphatically, moving for Keaton's arms at the exact same moment he stands to catch me.

Our mouths meet, and I kiss him as if it's the first time in a forever of kisses.

Friends and family cheer around us, and somewhere, someone pops champagne.

"I hope this was an okay proposal spot," Keaton whispers to me as our kiss ends, his lips trailing up my jaw and to my ear.

"I couldn't think of a better way." I breathe, in such shock that I need someone to pinch me.

And I really couldn't. To have the man I love ask me to marry him in the space that I'm hoping will bring so much happiness to my future ... it couldn't have been more perfect.

Keaton slides the ring onto my finger, and I stare at it in awe.

"We're getting married." I beam at him.

"You're going to officially be a Nash." He kisses me again.

"I'm going to have a daughter!" Eliza comes over, pulling me into a hug and I squeeze her back.

As we get separated for a while, both welcoming an onslaught of hugs and congratulations, I let the love in the room suffuse my soul. Eventually, we make our way back to each other, and Keaton pulls me to the far corner to have a little alone time.

When I survey the room, gazing over the special group who helped us both get to this place, my eyes catch on two people. Bowen and Lily, their bodies closer to each other than I'd ever seen them since I moved to Fawn Hill. Lily has her hand on his arm, and she looks like she's pleading with him. Meanwhile, Bowen is as icy as ever, staring at her with those dark blue eyes that give off this "either fuck you or fight you" vibe. It's actually kind of hot watching them ... the two have the chemistry of a box of fireworks. Illegal ones.

"Bowen and Lily talking? Are pigs flying over this building?" I look up at the ceiling, pretending I can see those animals with wings.

Keaton presses his forehead to mine. "He agreed to be civil today. I'll have to tell you that story some other time. But ... crazier things have happened. Like a city girl becoming a country mouse and agreeing to marry me."

From what it looks like, I wouldn't call their conversation civil. I would call it hushed, impassioned, tense ... but not civil. Something was going on between those two, and I'd get to the bottom of it a different day.

I sigh and snuggle farther into his embrace, pressing my cheek flat against his chest. "Yeah, I guess that is pretty crazy."

"Who would have thought, when you brought your underwear-eating dog in, that someday I'd put a ring on your finger?" Keaton chuckles.

A laugh bubbles up out of my throat. "Oh lord, Chance. I guess I owe that dog one, huh?"

Keaton bends down, pressing his lips to my ear. "You know what I'd like to have seen? You, in that pink thong."

A shiver moves over my skin. "I think we can do a little better than pink lace. Didn't I mention that under this pair of yoga leggings, I don't wear underwear?"

His body goes rigid and in the next instant he's dragging me by the hand toward the door of the studio.

Laughter bubbles in my throat as I dig in my heels and pull him back to me. Keaton catches me by the waist, looking at my ring as I place my hand on his chest.

"We have our whole lives ahead of us to leave parties early and touch each other inappropriately in corners." I smirk at him, raising an eyebrow. "Let's enjoy our friends and family while they're here."

He relents. "You're right. But get ready, we have an eternity of spontaneity, and settling, ahead of us."

Those two opposites had never sounded so right.

Those two opposites had never fit as perfectly as we did.

---

ondering what happened to Bowen and Lily? Read *Forgiven,* book two in the Nash brothers series! And here is a sneak peek ...

# Chapter 1

*Lily*

Smoke pours out from under the hood of my car, and a clap of thunder has me gently banging my forehead against the steering wheel.

"Why now?" I groan, asking the universe why my karma has gone from zilch to double zilch in the last ten minutes.

Of course, my brand new vehicle is breaking down on the side of the road right as it's about to storm. What a perfect metaphor for my life.

Okay, it's not that bad, I'm just being dramatic. But I'm tired after smiling and shaking hands at one of my father's rallies across county lines, and all I want to do is curl up on the over-sized couch in my townhouse living room with the most recent romance novel I checked out. Now, it looks like I'll be waiting for a tow truck instead of pulling on yoga pants.

The sky splits in a flash of light, right down the center, and not three seconds later does a boom from the heavens seem to shake the earth below my tires. The rain is threatening, and I dig in my bag for my phone to call Johnny at the garage I regularly use in Fawn Hill.

But the line just rings and rings, and either he's talking to every single resident of my small hometown, or I'm out of range. It's probably the latter, and I have to suck in a shaky breath to keep from crying.

Today has been trying. This week has been trying. Hell, the last ten years of my life have been trying. That's just how it goes when you are nowhere near where you expected to be at this age. At one time in my life, I thought that by twenty-eight, I'd be married with two children, watching from the stands as the only man I ever loved—

I have to mentally shut the images flooding my brain down. Now the tears do come, sharp and brutal, stinging my face just as equally as they're stinging my heart. How, after all of these years, I can still be such a mess over him ... it's the cruelest act of fate I've ever seen.

But, I'm a big girl now. I have my dream job; I run a local government entity, own my townhouse and have friends who love me for me. And hey, I negotiated with a car salesman last week to get this car down five thousand dollars in price. It may be malfunctioning now, but I'd worked hard to both save for this car and advocate for myself.

So, remembering that, I swallow my emotion and begin to call every garage or tow company within a twenty-five-mile radius. As I dial, the car gets worse; the smoke wafting over the hood and the smell of burning stinging my nostrils. I decide to get out of the car, just in case it blows up, and continue my quest for a tow.

I'm on garage number ten, whose voicemail I get when headlights come beaming in my direction. Another car! Thank heavens. Of course my car broke down on a backroad that even locals don't normally use, but I like the shortcut back from Lancaster ... and it's a bit like driving down memory lane.

The vehicle approaching is a truck, one of those monster things with tires as big as my torso and a bed that you could fit an entire football team into. Nighttime is fast upon us, and I can't make out the color as dusk sets in, but who cares.

I flag it down, attempting to point to my smoking car just in case the driver doesn't realize that I'm stranded out here. It's not likely that anyone from this part of Pennsylvania *won't* stop, but occasionally, you'll get a jerk or two.

The truck slows down, and my heart rate instantly picks up.

Because I know this truck.

Not intimately, it's been far too long for him to still have the same pickup he drove in high school. But I've seen it around town. It haunts my periphery, and whenever I spot it, I try to stay far away from it.

The driver cuts the engine, and then there he is. Climbing out in all of his giant, muscled glory.

My knees go weak, my mouth runs dry, my heart shakes unsteadily.

Bowen Nash has always been the most gorgeous male specimen to me, I never could take my eyes off of him. From the first time I saw him my freshman year of high school, the big, bad baseball-playing sophomore whose smile could charm a viper ... every other guy ceased to exist.

But now? He was a man in every sense of the word. And my lord, no man had ever done it better.

Broad, muscled shoulders led to arms thickly roped with hard-earned biceps and forearms. His chest alone was probably as long as my wingspan, and it led to a tapered waist where I imagined the steel-cut abs were smattered with hair darker than the close-cut fade that adorned his head. Not that I'd seen them in a very long time, but ...

Now he's walking toward me, those massive, sculpted thighs pressing against the fabric of his jeans as he maneuvers like a jungle cat. Bowen always has had that unteachable swagger to him.

I'm scared to look up into his face because that's the part that hooks my heart like a fish waiting to meets its doom. Powerless, that's what I am. The man's avoided me for ten years, and yet, if he confessed his love for me tomorrow, I'd go running back.

Sucking in a breath, I finally meet those blue eyes. The ones that gazed at me as we danced at prom. Those cerulean, almost translucent blue eyes that watched as I gave myself to him and only him, for what I thought would be forever. Bowen's eyes had looked at me through all the most important moments of our young lives ... and now, he barely swung them my way.

"Oh." He stops short once he sees it's me that he's jumped out of his chariot to rescue.

What he meant to say is, "oh, it's you," but the disdain in his tone still gets his message across.

I'm not sure where it all went wrong. My memories of that time are still fuzzy. All I do know is that we crashed and burned, both physically and in our relationship. And I ended up losing the love of my life for reasons he still won't reveal.

"My car broke down," I offer weakly, stating the obvious because I don't know what else to say.

Bowen looks at the smoking hood and walks past me, not even a flicker of kindness thrown my way. He pops the hood and disappears. After a few seconds, I round it, not able to stand here in his presence if he won't even speak to me.

"It's fine, I'm calling for a tow. You can go."

He ignores me. "I'm not a mechanic, but I'd say your radiator is busted. Is this ... someone else's car?"

The way he says it, he might as well ask if I'm seeing someone because his tone is so accusatory. As if he'd even care, which is the strangest part.

"It's new. I bought it last week."

"Someone took advantage of you." Bowen's gaze is unimpressed.

This treatment makes me want to cry as does almost every interaction with my ex-boyfriend. From high school sweethearts to practical strangers ... it was tragic.

And now, it was getting old. Jeez, it was far past old. It was ancient.

"I said, I'm fine. I'll handle it. You don't want to help, so go."

My tone has more bitterness in it than I thought I could possibly direct toward him.

Just as the words leave my mouth, the first of the rain starts to fall. Steadily pattering down onto us and the cars, I hold a hand up to cover my head. It does nothing, however, to remediate the sputtering under the hood of my car.

Bowen looks at the smoke, at me, and up at the rainy sky ... and sighs loudly.

"I can give you a ride."

No please, no real caring about the statement, no courtesy. "Yeah ... I think I'll pass."

My sarcasm must have pissed him off. "Get in the car, *Lily*."

The nails digging into my palms bite with pain. "I said I'm fine. Don't do me any favors now, *Bowen*."

Overhead, the sky cracks with lightning, one I can almost feel the electricity of on my face.

"I'm not leaving you out here to fry. Or worse, drown. Get in the car. I won't be the one blamed if you die."

His words shock us both to stillness ... and I realize he didn't think about what he was saying until it was already coming out of his mouth.

Because once upon a time, he *had* almost killed me.

I move before I can think again, running to the passenger side of his car. Bowen follows, a burly figure getting soaked as he angrily stomps through the rain.

The rain sluices the windshield as we drive in silence, the wipers batting it quickly, only for the watery curtain to appear seconds later. It might be cold and damp outside, but inside the cab of the truck, the humidity of our attraction, the chemical way we've always been pulled to each other ... it's scorching me.

This night isn't unlike that night ten years ago, the one that changed both of our courses forever. Rain, lightning, darkness closing in and country roads that bend too easily. Him in the driver's seat, me in the passenger seat. Some old Tim McGraw song on the radio.

Except we weren't those kids anymore, the ones who were wild and in love and thought the world couldn't tell them boo. Those teenagers had their whole lives ahead of them, and they expected to be living them together.

"Thank you," I croak out.

The truck passes the sign for Fawn Hill, Bowen navigating us through town. He ignores my sincerity. "You still stay with your parents?"

Of course, he wouldn't know that I bought my own place, finally, last year. We don't know each other anymore.

"No, I have a townhouse on Conover." I smile.

"I know the development." He hasn't looked at me since we got in the car.

Part of me was hoping he'd say he was proud of me, that he'd always believed I could be independent of my political father. But, like always, he says nothing.

Fawn Hill is deserted, most people are sitting down around the dinner tables with their families at this time. I take advantage of the darkness that's set in ... to stare at Bowen as he drives.

The set of his cheekbones, his eyebrows, his jaw ... they're all filled with so much fury.

As he pulls the car onto the one lane road that leads around the circle of my townhouse community, I direct him to a stop just outside my door.

When he only grunts a goodbye, I melt.

I forget that I wasn't the only one who lost everything in that accident.

My hand reaches for his face, my fingertips feeling over the rough of his barely there beard. It's more like five-o'clock shadow and is the exact same shade of the neat cut of his locks. The move must shock Bowen because his head whips to me, and the minute his eyes lock onto mine, I'm clued in on the tiniest shred of vulnerability.

He's opened the door just a crack, and I search his expression, finding only pain, and it breaks my heart open. Bowen always seems to know how to make my heart weep.

"I'll say it for the thousandth time, but I hope you hear me. I don't know what it is I did to make you hate me so much, but I'm sorry."

I slide out of the passenger seat and slam the truck door in frustration. The prickly sense of old scar tissue being cut open again stays with me for the rest of the week.

Read the rest of the Nash Brothers series!

## ALSO BY CARRIE AARONS

Do you want your **FREE** Carrie Aarons eBook?

All you have to do is **sign up for my newsletter**, and you'll immediately receive your free book!

**Then, check out all of my books, available in Kindle Unlimited!**

*Standalones*:

If Only in My Dreams

Foes & Cons

Love at First Fight

Nerdy Little Secret

That's the Way I Loved You

Fool Me Twice

Hometown Heartless

The Tenth Girl

You're the One I Don't Want

Privileged

Elite

Red Card

Down We'll Come, Baby

As Long As You Hate Me

On Thin Ice

All the Frogs in Manhattan

Save the Date

Melt

When Stars Burn Out

Ghost in His Eyes

Kissed by Reality

*The Prospect Street Series:*
Then You Saw Me

*The Callahan Family Series:*
Warning Track

Stealing Home

Check Swing

Control Artist

Tagging Up

*The Rogue Academy Series*:
The Second Coming

The Lion Heart

The Mighty Anchor

*The Nash Brothers Series*:
Fleeting

Forgiven

Flutter

Falter

*The Flipped Series*:
Blind Landing

Grasping Air

# ABOUT THE AUTHOR

Author of romance novels such as Fool Me Twice and Love at First Fight, Carrie Aarons writes books that are just as swoon-worthy as they are sarcastic. A former journalist, she prefers the love stories of her imagination, and the athleisure dress code, much better.

When she isn't writing, Carrie is busy binging reality TV, having a love/hate relationship with cardio, and trying not to burn dinner. She lives in the suburbs of New Jersey with her husband, two children and ninety-pound rescue pup.

Please join her readers group, Carrie's Charmers, to get the latest on new books, exclusive excerpts and fun giveaways.

You can also find Carrie at these places:
Website
Amazon
Facebook
Instagram
TikTok
Goodreads

Made in United States
North Haven, CT
04 January 2022

14219957R00157